LYING IN STATE

LYING IN STATE

JULIAN RATHBONE

G. P. Putnam's Sons

New York

G. P. Putnam's Sons
Publishers Since 1838
200 Madison Avenue
New York, NY 10016

First American Edition 1986

Library of Congress Cataloging-in-Publication Data

Rathbone, Julian, date.
  Lying in state.

  I. Title.
PR6068.A8L9   1986   823'.914   85-28293
ISBN 0-399-13156-6

Printed in the United States of America
1 2 3 4 5 6 7 8 9 10

Photoset and printed in Great Britain by
Redwood Burn Limited, Trowbridge, Wiltshire

1

The sky was metallically yellowish, modulating to bronze where snow-cloud gathered over distant mountains, the air cold, very cold, and the city unnaturally quiet. The queue, eight files wide, nudged its way down one side of the Plaza de España and into the Calle de Bailén. Its sound was eerie – thousands of feet shuffling, thousands of whispering voices like a forest of aspens when the wind first stirs. The frenzied clatter of sparrows in a berry-filled tree was an impertinence.

The faces were frightening, macabre: beneath fedoras, Homburgs, glossy feathers shaped like the wings of crows, behind black mists of lace, were white masks, eyes tearful or rheumy with the cold, with black scarves pulled up to lips that were mauve or slashed with red. There were few who were young, few who were poor, almost none you could look at and say he's a labourer, she's a factory hand.

A man, elderly like the rest but with a trimmer figure, seemed almost to have been extruded by the revolving door on to the top step of the Hotel El Príncipe. He pulled on black gloves, settled his hat. About sixty-five with a white, neatly cropped moustache above a generous mouth, gold-rimmed bifocals, he could be, you might think, a doctor, a lawyer, a conservative academic. The Príncipe is a very good, if conservative hotel. But the leather on the black shoes was cracked, the hems of the trouser legs frayed, the nap on what had once been, say twenty years earlier, a very expensive Scottish topcoat, a Crombie, was now worn smooth, to a shine in places. And his eyes, a pale blue, almost grey, were not lugubrious or mournful, and lacked the self-congratulatory sureness of most of those in front of him. They all knew they were doing the correct thing, were in the right place at the right time, were assisting history to mark the passing of an epoch. The elderly man, however, lacked all pompous certainty and his eyes, true windows of the soul, betrayed a terrible anxiety – terror even.

The queue filled one side of the carriageway. The other was kept open for traffic – little of it now, mostly black cars with flags or badges denoting importance which whispered, as such cars do, to and from the Palace. Police and Guardia Civil stood at intervals – the police in grey and red with peaked hats pulled over their eyes, black accoutrements, the Guardias in green and shiny black. As always they looked more relaxed than anyone else. Some of them, and it seemed a sort of sacrilege, smoked. But then they were the favourites, the ones who had wrapped up the Civil War in a terrible nationwide purge and been awarded from the lips of the Caudillo himself the title *Bienméritos* – the Well-Deserving.

As always someone wanted to talk to them – colleagues in plain clothes, informers, *agents provocateurs*, the political pimps on the fringes of repression. In this case two men, thirtyish, dressed in immaculate jeans with short black leather jackets, longish black hair, stood with one black-cloaked, black-hatted moustachioed Guardia on the corner opposite the hotel. They looked the sort of touts, part gypsy, who hang around the bull-rings, even occasionally appear in borrowed finery as *peones* to the less fashionable *espadas*, and they smoked with the Guardia, chatted quietly, snickered.

But one had his eye on the hotel steps and as the elderly gentleman moved forward he nudged his companion. Briefly they stood on their cigarettes, touched hands with

2

the Guardia, and moved away back up the queue until they were close.

The elderly gentleman's frightened eyes watched them; absurdly his bottom lip trembled and he had to hide the weakness with a gloved hand. Then with the determination of a suicide on a cliff-edge he stepped down out of the hotel entrance and with a murmur of apology slipped into the ranks of the mourners. None objected, though the faces of those immediately behind him expressed disapproval: if gentlemen from every hotel they passed did this instead of joining at the end, they'd never get to the Palace. The elderly man settled himself in the middle of the eightwide file and let his poorly shod feet whisper along the cobbles where once the tram-lines had been. Slowly they wheeled into Calle de Bailén and the two followers stood by a lamp-post. Insolently they watched him pass, and, when he had, casually they moved on to the next lamp-post to wait for him.

Barely half a kilometre away a gun began to thud again, and just out of time with it a church bell bled out a muffled clang.

Remorselessly the icy black lava flowed on, carrying the elderly gentleman with it between the gardens of the Plaza de Oriente and the side wall of the Palace. As it moved, in spite of the fear he felt and because of the dreary slowness of it all, he remembered the only other time he had done this – attended a lying-in-state. That time it had been for Evita. Eva María Duarte de Perón. The rite, he mused, is well named, the embalmed body being the final lie in a life of lies. A few tiny snowflakes no bigger than midges and as reluctant to settle danced a pavan above. The stream began the slow wheel into the Plaza de la Armería and the huge façade of the Palace came into view. *Tu seras mieux logé que moi*, Napoleon had said to his brother. A tiny smile lifted the corners of the elderly gentleman's mouth as he remembered this, then the terror flooded back. The marshalled queue of mourners was passing into the Palace by the large door used by tourists on the ground floor beneath the long balcony. Discretely it drifted out again by the two doors to either side of it beneath the criss-crossing sweep of marble balustrades. Two doors, two hunters, who had only to wait for him outside. What he had thought might be an escape was a trap.

He scarcely took in the red and gold banners trimmed with black bows that hung from the windows, the giant laurel wreaths that hung between them, the lines of troops in black and scarlet with silver helmets that looked as if they had been borrowed from the fire brigade. But he felt clearly enough the change in the temperature as they passed into the building and ambled slowly beneath the black-trimmed chandeliers towards the magnificent staircase.

Four men stood at the foot of it – and his fear tightened even further, for they appeared to be scrutinising each file as it passed them. One was a general in uniform, the others were middle aged, in suits, with hard grim faces. As the elderly gentleman raised his foot for the first step two of them raised their right arms, casually it seemed, bent at the elbow, the palms flat, the fingers stretched. The man beside him returned the salute, as if acknowledging a wave from a friend. Only then did the elderly gentleman note the tiny enamel black, white and red swastika in his neighbour's buttonhole. The sight of it spiced his fear with nausea.

The underlying hysteria of the occasion began to cause cracks in the stucco façades of those around him. Old ladies with sticks paused and gasped on the steps, shallow though they were; the elderly gentleman noticed a flow of tears that ran gently as if from a partially opened faucet down the face of the yet more elderly gentleman on his other side. Black-edged handkerchieves appeared and carried with them the odours of cologne. Two files above him, just at the top of the staircase, perhaps just as the catafalque and casket came into view down the vista of state departments, or at any rate the candelabra at its corners, another old man paused, choked, sank to his knees, and toppled over; uniformed attendants came to his side, lifted him skilfully, carried him gently, off, out, and away.

It was a sign.

The terror faded a little. An excitement, perhaps even an elation replaced it. His gaze flickered about now, relishing for a moment Tiepolo's *Apotheosis of Aeneas*, and then at last they were there. A waxy face with rouged cheeks, eyelids not quite tight shut so you thought they might open, a well-clipped moustache not unlike his own, a nose beakier than he had expected jutting up from a cocoon of white satin, ribbons of red silk and gold, gold epaulets, a uniform black or deepest blue, and all concealing the awful ruin beneath. Inexorably the elderly gentleman was moved on and perhaps it was not so difficult after all to stumble and sink to the floor in a faint as convincing as any the attendants had yet seen.

Smelling salts and cologne were not enough – he saw to that. Oxygen he felt would do and when that was administered he opened his eyes to find himself in a small room lined with cased bookshelves, and old sepia photographs from the nineteenth century set on ugly tables, one signed *Victoria R*, leather chairs. Two nurses fussed over him, helped him to his feet. Carefully he let his knees relax. He lived, he said, in Recoletos, just off Velázquez, had come by Metro to Opera, but it was too far to walk, and the Metro was hell, so many people, so many people. They were concerned. If he would wait, they said, ten minutes, they would find a car, a vehicle of some sort . . . Too kind, too kind. *De nada, de nada*, so many brave old people have come, the nurses murmured, and the weather so cold.

It was a lie that he lived in Recoletos, just off Velázquez. Intelligent assessment of his shoes and cuffs would have made that clear. A large number of the people who had queued with him had come from that quiet expensive area of Madrid, but he had not. When the grey Land-rover of the Municipal Police, threading its way through the disconsolate city, reached Puerta del Sol the elderly gentleman asked the driver to bear left to José Antonio. The policeman was puzzled. 'It's quicker by Alcalá.'

'Of course. But... ' the elderly gentleman prevaricated, '... I have a sister. I should visit her. She is older than I, she will be distressed.'

He was dropped where he wanted, just by the Telefónica Building. The policeman obsequiously accepted his thanks, accepted his apparent status as one of the conservative well-to-do citizens he was paid to protect. The elderly gentleman watched the Land-rover turn, took in the fact that people were still drifting up Gran Vía towards what must be the end of the queue for a view of the cadaver in the Palace, then he was gone – up the alley by the side of the splendid, neo-baroque Telephone Building, Madrid's first sky-scraper.

This took him into a short, narrow street with high nineteenth-century tenements on both sides... Calle del Desengaño, the street of the Disenchanted Gentleman. It was almost deserted – no sign yet of the hunters. Briskly he crossed the road, entered a door which advertised a *pensión*, then climbed, with breath beginning to be a burden, heart pounding but forcing himself on for he knew he might be late, too late, up four flights of stairs. The steps of the first three flights were brass edged, the walls papered in raised acanthus design, purple flecked with gold. But the last flight, which climbed beyond the domain of the *pensión*, was plain, grubby but lighter. There was a skylight at the top.

He fingered his latchkey into the lock just to the right of the pale patch in the brown varnished door from which he had removed an image of the Sacred Heart, and pushed.

Darkness and no sound, except that of trickling water.

He cleared his throat.

'Ramón?'

No noise, except trickling water.

'Ramón? Are you there?'

He took a deep breath, fumbled for the light. It clicked, but nothing happened. He went on in, found a second switch, and again nothing. Back at the door he groped for the electricity metre and junction box. Its cut-out button was out. He pressed it in. Something cracked and flashed to his left and the button jumped out again.

'The Devil!' he said, in English.

He moved to his right, pushed open a door. Grey, dim light. He opened a second door and a little more light from the windows of the Telefónica almost opposite filtered in. Now he could see a thickish old-fashioned grey flex snaking from a porcelain two-pin power socket and on into the room to his right, the bathroom. He pulled out the plug, returned to the cut-out switch, and pressed it. Two lights came on – one in the hall and one in the bathroom.

The bathroom was tiny – one small window venting the gas-heater into the *patio de luces* – the centre well of the building – a bath, a basin, a lavatory, a terrazo floor that cunningly sloped to a small hole in the wall. If the floor got wet you could push the water out through it and it splashed down four storeys into the area below. It was needed now. The small bath was gently overflowing, a slow trickle, the cold tap had been left on.

In it was the appliance that ended the flex, a small, round, electric fire of the sort poorer Madrileños use under a table. The table is draped with a cloth that reaches to the floor, and you sit with your legs under it and your feet possibly touching the rim of the fire. In the old days the bowls were filled with charcoal instead of an electric element.

With it in the small bath was the body of a tallish man. His feet were submerged, his knees were bent above the level of the water, and his head lolled back over the rim. The body was thin, ascetic, an El Greco Piéta. This contrasted with the face which was solid and heavy, the lips thick and brick-red. Glossy black hair was slicked back from a broad forehead. It all had an eerily exact appearance of Juan Domingo Perón, the President of Argentina who had

7

died sixteen months earlier. But this face, which was a latex mask, did not look dead, not as dead even as the rouged Caudillo in the Palace, not as dead as the body on which it sat.

The elderly gentleman gasped, retched violently from an almost empty stomach over the lavatory bowl. His spectacles dropped in. He retrieved them, wiped them, and his face, on a small towel, and then staggered into the tiny and very dirty kitchen where he found a bottle of Osborne brandy. It had that wretched device on top that can limit the rate of flow and he shook it twice before he had as much as he wanted in a tall, straight Duralex glass. He drank it off, shuddered, nearly vomited again, then, recalling his situation, moved quickly back into the hall to check the door was locked. With his chest heaving as if air were coal he dragged and pushed and dragged an enormous wardrobe that stood against the back wall of the tiny hall until it was across the doorway. Metal coat-hangers jangled inside.

He then went into the one of the two living-rooms that was his and slumped into a low basketwork chair and waited until he had his breath back.

The room contained that one chair, a table improvised from composition board placed over a frame made from metal strips, bookshelves made in the same way, and a narrow bed with iron ends. There were also a small radio, two tape-recorders – one spool-to-spool, one cassette, and under the bed there were three battered suitcases. Two of these were filled with paperback books, and one with clothes – clean at one end, soiled at the other. The table was littered with books, tapes, and papers that almost buried a small typewriter. On the walls there was only one small decoration – a poster for a play – Los Peroles with caricatured portraits of Perón and Evita.

He hoisted the heavy grey tape-recorder on to the table, took off its lid, threaded up six-centimetre spools, and plugged in a large, stand-up microphone. He counted aloud, checked the bobbing needle for level, took a breath, and began.

'*Yo, Roberto Constanza y Fairrie...* '

There was a knock on the front-door, then a pounding. He froze for a moment, switched off the tape, crossed to one of the bookshelves and from behind the third volume of the collected works of V. I. Lenin took a very small silver .22 pistol. He pulled back the breech to cock it and then took up a position in front of the barricade he had erected. But the pounding stopped. Then footsteps, two pairs, receded down the wooden stairs. Roberto looked down at the pistol in his hand and sighed as if a burden of guilt and shame had suddenly fallen on his weary shoulders. He crossed the tiny hall to the other living-room – the same as his, furnished in much the same way, but with one feature different – where his had a table used as a desk this had a dressing-table with a triptych of mirrors and drawers beneath. On the top were sticks of stage make-up, false hair, spirit gum, powder and so on, rags and vanishing cream.

Roberto sat in front of it, looked at his reflection in the centre mirror, and the doubled reflections of his profile in the side mirrors, then sat back to avoid them. Tears suddenly flowed. He waited until they ceased, wiped his eyes on one of the rags, then wrapped the pistol in it before slipping it into the top left-hand drawer. Again the sigh.

He stood, looked out of the window. He could just see the street corner below. A man in a leather jacket, collar turned up, was lighting a cigarette. The elderly gentleman returned to his own room, switched on the tape-recorder and began again.

'I, Robert Constance Fairrie... '

Distantly the guns banged away for the last time that day as darkness slowly thickened outside and the tiny snowflakes that would not settle danced like fireflies in the light from the Telefónica, and beneath the street lamps.

2

'I, Robert Constance Fairrie, feel I need to make a statement. A statement about who I am and about how I came to be in the situation I am now in. My life is in danger. A very dear friend of mine has been murdered, yet in circumstances which could be interpreted to show that I was the murderer. Similarly a respected colleague was gunned down on my doorstep less than twenty-four hours ago and people malevolent towards me as well as towards him could uncover a credible if false motive that might indicate that I was the culprit. Most easy of all I suppose would be for them to contrive my death to look like suicide and then make sure that blame for the two previous murders was lain, laid, at my door. So. I have good reasons to make this statement. Which will be as full and accurate as I can make it . . . '

He pressed the stop button, returned to the kitchen, shook more brandy into the glass, peeled open a small tin of sardines, and ate them with a piece of stale bread cracked from a stick loaf. Then he drank the brandy and returned to his room.

'My name is Roberto Constanza y Fairrie, Robert Constance Fairrie, and I was born in Buenos Aires in 1910. My father was an insurance underwriter and a well-to-do, even wealthy person. He sent me to a refined and progressive public school in England, St George's, Harpenden, and from there I went to Cambridge...'

Again the stop button. Roberto waited for a moment then pulled off his spectacles, wiped them, put them on again, and restarted the machine.

'But this is not biography. Merely my account of recent tragic events in which I have been involved. Not biography, but certain ... moments in my past have relevance.

'In the late forties and early fifties I was active in both the socialist and communist parties of my country and ran, not for profit of course, a bookshop where political pamphlets and books were sold. In April 1953 this shop was destroyed by fire. A fascist mob inspired by a deliberately inflammatory speech – the adjective is exactly apt – from the President, Juan Domingo Perón, was responsible. I narrowly escaped with my life and I still have burn scars. I should add that the same mob also burned the headquarters of both the socialist and radical parties as well, and made a complete job of it with the Jockey Club, the meeting place of the conservative oligarchy. Anyone who opposed Perón was in danger. Outside my shop they chanted "Jew, go home to Moscow", and, worse still, "Juden rause".

'I have a little Jewish blood. Very little by now. The Fairries were, I think, originally Portuguese Jews who settled in England in the sixteenth century. Though I have to say my grandmother insisted that the original was a good Catholic washed up on the shores of Scotland after the Armada. Her version has it that he married a daughter of the Duke of Montrose. By the nineteenth century they were sugar importers based in Liverpool. One of them came to Buenos Aires with the growth of sugar cultivation in the north of Argentina, and his daughter was my mother. My father, Giovanni Pablo Constanza was an insurance broker... this is not relevant, I will try to be relevant, from an Italian, Genovese family of bankers. His mother was Spanish Argentinian, as was the mother of my mother...

'I must keep to the point. After the burning of my shop I left Argentina and used my private means to run similar ventures in other countries. But I am an historian by training. During my exile I used my skills to research the Perón phenomenon and track the history of that man's rise and fall and extraordinary return to power. Occasionally I published articles in academic journals, though rarely, since I was not attached to any academic institution. Nor did I wish to be.

'It would not be a lie to say that I am now in impoverished circumstances and have been so for some time. My disposable capital has been exhausted to further the collapse of Capital. Ha! However, a careful grandfather entailed much of his fortune and I still receive quarterly cheques from a trust managed by what has now become the Bank of London and South America. These, the cheques I mean, are meagre. Perhaps my grandfather should not have invested quite so heavily in Anglo-Argentinian Tramways.

'Sixteen months ago Perón died. I felt I was in a position to prepare and produce a biography. I worked on a synopsis for some months and tried to sell it to various publishers, both Hispanic and English. Although I had taken pains to make the work one of objective history it was always refused... I sensed for political reasons.'

Just the pause button this time, held down while he collected his thoughts.

'I have, for a long time, admired the journalism, the "in-depth" journalism, of Steve Cockburn, formerly of the *Sunday Times*. I have read his books with enthusiasm, and often wished that I had been in a position to see his television series on South American dictatorships entitled "Where Next will the Lightning Strike?".

'Not only is he very well-informed concerning South America but clearly too he has connections in the media world of the United Kingdom. And so, about five months ago, I sent him my synopsis of a life of Perón. After five weeks or so he answered, not too encouragingly, but raising points of criticism that I felt I should answer. A sporadic correspondence ensued, which, a month ago, I believed had been terminated on both sides with mutual respect.

'I was therefore rather surprised when I...'

The stop button again. The elderly gentleman stood up and lurched out into the hall, hand groping for the bathroom door. He stopped, swung instead into the kitchen, unzipped and peed into the oily sink. He then made himself black espresso coffee, using a hand-grinder and a small pressurised pot. While the process went on he found a pack of Peter Stuyvesant on one of the shelves, shook one out, lit it from a screwed spill of paper pushed into the gas jet, inhaled deeply, coughed rackingly and threw it too into the sink. He poured his coffee into a green octagonal cup, added a small amount of Osborne, and carried it back to his room. There he wound the tape back a metre or so, listened to his own voice, nodded to himself, drank *café y coñac*, and reset the machine to 'record'.

'I was therefore rather surprised when I received a cable from Steve Cockburn. It ran as follows...'

Again the stop, and a search lasting four minutes over and under his table before he found the right piece of paper.

'It ran as follows...' The paper crackled as he spread it out. '"Urgentest we meet. Arriving Barajas 11.45. 11.11.75. Cockburn."...'

3

On 11 November Roberto took the bus to the airport.
It was a bright, dry day trying to be warm, the frost reluctant to leave the shade, snow twinkling in the violet Gua-
darramas. He enjoyed a trip out to the airport, took one
occasionally if funds allowed, just for the hell of it, to sit in
the lounge and sip cold beer from the self-service, or dry
sherry with manzanilla olives. There he would watch the
big jets storming in and storming out, the sad departures
and passionate arrivals, would guess 'What's My Line?' for
the silver heads with gilt locks on their briefcases and male
secretaries in tow. Once he too had travelled in style, and
while he had no hankering for it now, or regret that his
money had gone (apart that is from feeling unused without
a radical bookshop to run), he liked to remind himself of it
all.

So that day in November, and very much aware of an
extra *frisson* of excitement, very conscious that in an hour
or so he would be taking a step into the unknown, into a
situation which was unclear to say the least, he arrived half
an hour early – which, allowing for passenger clearance
was a good hour early, and ordered himself a *coñac*.
Brandy for heroes. The plane was late – fog at Heathrow –
and by the time Cockburn came through the gates into the
arrival area at one o'clock, Roberto was a little tipsy.

Cockburn was drunk. He came through the doors like

a bull out of the *toril* and paused four yards out, blinking and tossing his head. He was tall and thin, not really bull-like at all, with very coarse hair nearly grey, a face a bit jowly and running to seed and at this moment very dissipated, with a sheen of alcoholic perspiration across a brow whose hue would not have disgraced a lily or a morgue. He was dressed in a white shirt, open at the top with a gold Christopher peeping through white and black hair, an expensive soft leather jacket in Cordoban red, tailored stretch jeans and shin-high cowboy boots that matched the jacket. A porter behind him pushed a trolley on which were two battered hide suitcases. With the arrogance of a media person he had not bothered to send Roberto any means of identification, but Roberto clutched a copy of *Up the Plate without a Paddle* which had a large Jerry Bauer portrait of Cockburn on the back, and it was accurate enough.

'Mr Cockburn?'

'Yes?' Puzzled.

Together: 'I am Roberto Fairrie... ' 'You must be Roberto Constanza... '

'Yes indeed. But actually I usually drop the Constanza.'

'*Muy bien. Bueno. ¿Qué tal, Señor Fairrie?*'

'Very well. But it is not necessary to talk in Spanish. My English is adequate.'

'Better than mine, old chap.'

'Did you have a good journey, Mr Cockburn?'

'Horrible. A nightmare. Call me Steve. Which way do we go?'

'You would like a taxi?'

'You don't have a car?'

'Actually no. I find the traffic in Madrid too daunting at my age.'

'Well then a taxi.'

They trundled out into the acid sunshine and blinked like bats. The taxi-driver wanted to know where he was to take them.

15

'You have an hotel?'

'Not booked.'

Silence. The taxi-driver waited.

'I usually stay at the Príncipe.'

'I am sure they will not be full at this time of year.'

They began the bleak descent into the piny suburbs of north Madrid and the jets thundered across the blue sky above them.

'I am sorry you had a bad journey.'

'Well. Had a bit of a party last night, and, I tell no lie, I wasn't too sure what plane I was on or where it was going. This has happened to me. I have one of these credit cards just for air travel and once, you know, I damn well woke up in Tokyo.

'Anyway, there I was, the stewardess prodding me and giving me coffee and these mountains below, a bit of snow on them, and we were coming down. Ankara? Santiago? No, the trip hadn't lasted long enough, there had been no stops on the way. Then just as I was about to make a fool of myself and ask, there was one of those great black Osborne bulls in a field, and, do you know it all came back to me in a flash, just like that.'

Roberto was curious.

'That's most interesting,' he said. 'You really got on that plane without knowing what you were doing? What about your luggage?'

Cockburn leant forward, elbow on knee, rubbed his forehead between forefinger and thumb.

'Well, yes. I suppose so. Must have packed or Sarah packed for me. Sarah's the living-in girlfriend of the moment. Then gone to the party. Dash it, I don't normally go on business trips in gear like this. I do hope the dear girl had the sense to put in a decent suit and a tie. Probably not. I do rather feel she wanted to come and I wouldn't let her. Hopefully, there's nooky waiting for me in Madrid. Then she must have bunged me in a taxi with a label round my neck and told the cabbie to pass me on to Iberia reception at Heathrow. Jolly decent of everyone to get it right.'

The black and yellow Seat cab continued past the ugly new ministry buildings and Generalísimo became the Paseo de la Castellana.

'Business?' said Roberto.

'Eh?'

'You are here on business.'

'Yes. You could say that. Christ. I haven't told you, have I? I mean I haven't told you why I'm here, why I asked you to meet me.'

'No.'

'Christ. Jolly decent of you to turn up then. Just on spec.'

'I rather hoped... that my history of Peronismo, my biography synopsis...'

'Well yes. I mean actually in a way it is to do with that. But not quite. I mean I would not want to raise your hopes at all, but at the same time I do rather think you can do me a favour in that line, and well, I might be able to offer you a quid pro quo. Perhaps even more than a quid...' He stopped, glanced sideways at Roberto. Had the old geezer understood the joke? Christ, yes. And by golly we are not amused.

The taxi halted, then inched forward in a long double queue of jammed traffic. The cabbie swore – the rebuilding of the square at Colón was the reason, a crazy enterprise full of underground shops, theatres no one would ever use.

'Look. It's quite a complicated matter. It really is. And quite honestly I don't feel up to explaining it to you yet... Goodness. Did you see the graffiti on that hoarding? *Viva El Rey.* Long live the King. Is it that close?'

'Very close. Tomorrow, the day after. No one expects it to be much longer.'

'What then?'

Roberto shrugged but said nothing. He thought: *Operación Lucero* was spoken of. The night Franco died it was said all dissidents, lefties, Basques, communists, what-

17

ever, would be rounded up. Put in the bull-rings. The football stadia. Pinochet had shown the way in Chile. He spoke at last.

'¿*Quién sabe?*'

Cockburn nodded: 'Who knows?'

The taxi broke out of Colón at last and the traffic streamed on to Cibeles with its extraordinary statue of a pagan goddess and wedding cake joke of a central post office. Shortly they were in Gran Vía, or, as the street signs called it but almost no one else, Avenida de José Antonio.

'Anyway. As I was saying. It really was jolly decent of you to meet me. I'm really not up to explaining it all to you now. But I do think you should know there really will be something in it for you – I mean, I'm pretty sure you can be of real service to me, and of course I'll pay the going rate.'

Traffic lights again.

'Listen. Are you free this evening?'

'Yes.'

'Well. Let's see. Why not meet me for dinner? By then I should be feeling a bit more up to it.'

'All right. If you say so.'

'I can see you're a bit peeved. Quite understand. But just as of now I'm not up to it.'

'All right. Dinner.'

'Yes. Um . . . Do you know a restaurant called El Cid? Not far from the Opera?'

'I know it.'

'Nine o'clock there. Then.'

They were outside the Callao Metro station – not far from Desengaño.

'I'll get out here.'

'*Hasta la vista.*'

'Yes.'

4

'I must confess my first meeting with Steve Cockburn had been something of a disappointment. It was not just, or indeed mainly because my hopes had been raised of a contract to continue my work on Perón, but that he seemed to be more in the mould of the conventional British journalist – a drunk in short – than I had expected. His reputation as an acute observer of our times, particularly well-informed about Latin-American affairs, had blinded me to the possibility that his actual character, his personality, might lack weight. Though reflecting on it during that afternoon, and indeed dipping again into the three books of his I have on my shelves, one could not help noticing now a certain superficiality in his approach to, say, Argentinian politics. For instance, in *Up the Plate without a Paddle* he ascribes too much importance to Perón's dalliance with nubile girls following the death of Evita. Perón's fall was due far more to historical objective circumstances and his own bizarre failure to read the way history works.

'With these reflections and others like them I amused myself for the rest of that day, and of course speculated too on what had brought Cockburn to Madrid and on what way he believed I could help him. And, I must confess, just

19

what sort of fee he would be paying. More than a quid. A silly joke.

'I must say, too, I looked forward with keen anticipation to a meal at El Cid. It is not in the very top rank of Madrileño restaurants, but perhaps deserves a higher reputation than it has. One should not be put off by all the Hollywood-style decorations, accoutrements and so on that fill the walls: shields, lances, and even suits of armour, that sort of thing. The food is good and contrives, without too much neglect of decent kitchen practice, to retain an authentically Spanish style. In short, it is not international cuisine.

'Cockburn, I was glad to see, had found a reasonable suit in his baggage ... '

'Fish soup for you then, followed by the broiled lamb. You're sure? First day back in Madrid I tend to go for the fishy specialities. You know, one of those towers piled and hung with Dublin Bay prawns, crabs, crayfish. But they never do them for one person only.'

But Roberto was determined. Quite often he bought fish in the market behind the Plaza Mayor, but hardly ever meat, and never the larger cuts – with only two gas rings he lacked the means to cook them properly even if he could have afforded them.

'I think you will find the lamb equally typical, indeed more typical of Castile. And as you see, for two people we can share a leg.'

A whole leg of lamb – tougher, smaller, and leaner than you buy in England – but marinated for at least two days to tenderise it, then spit roast ...

'Well, I'll leave it to you then.' This said a touch petulantly. 'And the wine?'

Roberto looked over the wine list.

'Castillo Sant'Simon from Jumilla is not as well known as the Riojas, but I think you'll find it acceptable.'

'It's dearer than the Riojas.'

Roberto shrugged. 'Let's have a fino to begin with. Manzanilla de San Lúcar for me, if they've got it.'

Cockburn crumbled snow-white powdery bread and leant back, eyeing Roberto over the candles. After a long afternoon sobering up, bathing, shaving, he looked now more of a personality. His face had lost its pallor, had the sheen one associates with a combination of evil living and healthy exercise – no doubt he swam and played squash in a club like the RAC. Roberto himself had been able to do just that during the three years he ran a bookshop in Rathbone Place. The suit was dark charcoal, flared jacket, two vents, the waistcoat a Liberty damask – much the fashion of the late sixties but it had style still and did a lot for a man of Cockburn's age. Roberto estimated him to be just about fifty. The Englishman's eyes glittered in the light which added something a touch Mephisophelean to his expression.

'I imagine you'd like to know something of what this is all about.'

Roberto assented.

'Well. It's a longish story, but it starts with Juan Domingo Perón in exile in Madrid from 1960 to 1973. He was made welcome here and the first years were much eased by the presence and renewed friendship of the actress Nini Montiam. You have heard of her?'

'Of course. I actually saw her perform in Buenos Aires in the early fifties. She was a good friend of Perón's and Evita's. Here in Madrid she has run, used to run a rather good little theatre where one could sometimes see pieces not usually permitted by the regime. She enjoyed the protection of a general I believe.'

Cockburn frowned slightly. 'All right, you know who Montiam is.'

He drank some soup, picked a tiny shellfish off his spoon, sucked out the meat and dropped the shell on the side plate.

21

'Well, while Perón was here, he was bored for much of the time, especially early on, and he amused himself by recording his reminiscences on tapes. In the end there were over one hundred and forty hours of them. Apparently he just sat there and rapped...'

'Rapped?'

'Improvised – made it up as he went along. And they contained amazing stuff, were entertaining, revealing. Never intended for publication, he was just having a ball. And when he left in '73 he just gave them to Montiam, a thank-you present not to be used until he was dead. And of course back in Buenos Aires he barely lasted a year.'

'Just over.'

'Eh?'

'Just over. About fifty-five weeks.'

'Ah. Anyway he died. Not long after that, six months or so, Montiam put them on the market, just about a year from where we are now, in fact told Becky Herzer that she had them and that they were up for sale...'

'Becky Herzer?'

'Well, I don't suppose you'd know of her. She's Czech by birth, family got out in '48, she's now French. Most of her life she's spent in France, first as a journalist, then doing TV work, now operates as a freelance independent producer, wrapping up deals with publishers and newspapers too. Very international. She knew Montiam, Montiam told her about the tapes, and Becky got in touch with me. Old pals, often worked together, and she felt she needed someone on board with a bit more spic clout than she had. Latin-American.'

'I know what "spic" means.'

'Quite. I say this wine is jolly good. Almost porty. Let's hope the lamb lives up to it.'

'I'm sure it will.'

'Where was I? Yes. Becky then called me in. I came over, we went to Montiam's and heard some extracts from the tapes and I realised we were on to something really big. Yes, very big.'

Cockburn smiled, almost coyly: like a spoilt boy, Roberto thought, a spoilt boy admitting to over-indulgence in candy but knowing no one will really mind.

'Why *big*?'

'Why not?'

'Because most politicians' memoirs are a bore. Anything Perón ever wrote was plagiarised or ghosted. He was not renowned for his ability to tell the truth.'

'Oh quite, quite so.'

Cockburn seemed disposed to sulk at this rebuff, drank soup noisily, until the leg of lamb, a rich dark brown and spitted, on what looked like a medieval poniard, arrived. Brandy was heated, slopped on, lit. The head waiter held the flaring limb aloft.

'I rather like my lamb well done,' Cockburn said nervously.

'Then you should have the knuckle end,' said Roberto with something like glee. The other end was meatier.

By the time it was all done, and all the trappings served too, and Cockburn had pronounced himself very well pleased, he was ready to take up his story again.

'You see, there was no question of ghosting this time. It was Perón's voice all right, and much of what he said was sensational.'

'Really?'

'Really. On Evita's morals. US intervention in Latin-American domestic affairs. The imbecility of every politician who ever opposed him . . . '

'That at any rate was to be expected.'

'Of course. Also a do-it-yourself kit on how to turn a radical union into a bunch of *lazzaroni*. And there was other stuff too.' Cockburn slipped a morsel of lamb between over-white teeth that Perón himself would have been proud of, leant forward and tapped the side of his nose. 'Nazi *émigrés* in Argentina.'

Roberto's face remained expressionless. 'Did you hear any of that?'

'Not actually. But Nini said it was there.'

They ate on, Roberto drank some of the Castillo Sant'Simon, and said: 'So?'

'Well. All this you understand is preamble as to why you and I are here as of now.' Again, already, Roberto thought, he is tipsy. 'So I will move as quickly as I can through the ensuing sequence. Which won't be difficult since it definitely left me with egg on my face and that is not something I like to dwell on. Montiam wanted two hundred grand, dollars, down, no frills. For that we could have the tapes and do what we liked with them. I realised she'd got it about right. With translations, serial rights, maybe a TV spin-off, the whole shoot, I could see the project netting about two million. Becky and I reckoned we should take about fifty grand each.

'We started off, Becky and I, doing it the conventional way. We took it to a mainline Latin-American/Spanish publisher, of high repute but with a bit of devil in him. He has a fat rich business, comics and girlie magazines at the base, Althusserian Marxism at the tiny tip. He was enthralled, but nervous...'

Cockburn too was enthralled by the magic of his tale. He leant back, leant forward, flourished a fork, then a knife, swigged from his glass and ordered another bottle.

'Enthralled but nervous. He decided to set up an entirely new company to handle the merchandise, keeping himself in the background. Nervous but ready to put up a very handy lump sum... A handy lump sum,' he repeated with relish. 'We really thought we were laughing. And then...'

'And then?'

'Just two days later he pulled out. No reason. He just rang up and said no deal. This happened two more times. I won't give you the details but one drama–doc producer we're both very friendly with, said he'd actually been leant on by some very nasty characters indeed.

'That happened in Geneva where our search for finance had taken us, and that brings me to Peter Clemann. Clemann is a US exile: won't make the necessary statements about his political associations to get back his US passport. He is also a multi-millionaire. About seventy million the last time he had it counted. And he lives in Geneva, and he is a very old and dear friend of mine. How that came about I'll tell you another day. Not too relevant just now. Well, since we were in Geneva, where we had drawn a blank, I went to see him, told him what we were up to and he said he'd back us. So we all met up here in Madrid, which Peter hates, for him Spain is the arse-hole of Europe, Madrid the... We all sat down in the Príncipe, and it really did seem that this time we were OK. No one leans on Clemann. He's fireproof. Again we were laughing.' He leant back, drank deeply, refilled his glass. His dark eyes glittered. Then he swung back to what was left of his lamb.

'Even so,' – waving a fork so Roberto feared a blob of gravy in his eye – 'there were unbelievable difficulties. Becky turned out to be against Jews and millionaires and hated Clemann on sight. But the main thing was Nini seemed terrified we were planning some fiddle – like walk off with the tapes leaving her with a rubber cheque, that sort of thing. It got to be very complicated indeed. But in the end we had it right, notorised cheques for Nini, arrangements to everyone's satisfaction for transfer, deeds drawn up ready to be signed. Of course we knew there were people in the background who were trying to ditch us. I'd even thought heavies in macs were tailing us, but never managed to prove it. Peter heard from Geneva that shady characters had been trying to pry into his affairs. But he was determined. He had machines flown in from Geneva that would duplicate the tapes, transfer them to miniature cassettes as soon as we had the title. Then each of us was to take a copy and fly out be different routes. We had thought of everything. And then literally at the last moment everything went wrong.'

'I know.'

'Know what?'

'Everything went wrong. It's public knowledge.'

'I'm sorry. I'm really not with you.'

Roberto sighed, pushed his crumpled napkin on to the table. Cockburn allowed himself to be aware of the waiter at his elbow.

'Afters?'

'I think I do dare to eat a peach.'

'Very droll. I'll have a rum baba with a dollop of chantilly. Now tell me just what is public knowledge.'

Roberto took off his spectacles, gave them a polish on the napkin, slipped them back on.

'I have,' he said, 'a friend who reads *ABC*. I'm afraid I don't. I'm sure you know it is a right-wing monarchist review. But my friend knows of my interest in Perón and he drew my attention to an announcement that was made in *ABC* some time ago. The magazine – or I suppose we must say its bank or whatever – had bought from an unnamed party tapes of reminiscences left here by Perón. No reason not to suppose that they were referring to the ones you were negotiating for. Planeta, who have connections with *ABC* will publish sometime next year. There is to be a small team of editors supervised by Señor Luca de Tena who is the editor of *ABC*. I imagine that at the last moment they made Señora Montiam an offer she could not refuse.'

'Well, I'm damned. Of course we knew it was *ABC* who was fronting for whoever bought the tapes but we never expected them ever to publish. Quiet suppression is what we expected.'

'Oh yes. They'll publish. Under the title *Yo, Juan Domingo Perón*.'

'But edited.'

'Of course.'

'So all the dirt cut out.'

'You don't have to assume that. Listen, Mr Cockburn,

26

Perón was bombastic, conceited, a congenital liar... it would be easy for any slandered person to shrug off what he said. Only very hard, verifiable, yet previously unknown fact would do anyone any real damage.'

5

Cockburn suddenly contrived to appear very serious indeed.

'Hard, verifiable, previously unknown fact.'

'Yes.'

'Like the whereabouts of Martin Bormann?'

Roberto nodded slowly, began slowly to peel his peach. 'Yes,' he said. 'That would have impact.'

'The exact details of how the US State Department engineered the ouster of October '46 and then bungled the aftermath so Perón was elected?'

'Rather old hat now... but people do like reading about proved instances of American intervention. Especially when they are incompetently executed.'

'How about this: the sexual relationship between Evita and her brother Juan. How brother Juan gave her the syphilis she really died of, and thus why Perón countenanced or ordered his murder.'

'Oh come on. Come on.' Roberto's incredulity seemed for a moment forced, but the laugh that followed was clearly unfeigned. 'And that's hard, verifiable fact?'

'Perhaps not. But if you heard Perón himself say it, you'd be ready to believe it. And there are millions both of the right and the left who would love to hear him say it, and pay to hear him say it.'

Roberto drank the last of his wine. 'And you have

heard him say it. This is what you heard on Montiam's tapes and what you believe *ABC* and Planeta will suppress.'

'Oh no.' Cockburn's face swam further into the candlelight. 'Oh dear me no. You see, old boy, it's not that first lot of tapes that brings me to Madrid. Not at all. What brings me now to Madrid is the existence of a second lot of tapes.'

Roberto sank back. His head was swimming. Though he was used to drink he had had a fair bit, and a long heavy meal. It had not been easy, either, listening to Cockburn's drawn-out tale, waiting for the punch-line.

'A... ah-h.' It was more a sigh than an exclamation. 'A second lot of tapes. And where have they sprung from?'

'That I'm not quite sure of. But of course I know who has them now.'

Roberto waited.

'At this point I must introduce one of the main characters in the whole episode.'

Roberto looked round nervously, but it was a figure of speech merely.

'Pepa. Josefina González. Pepita. She, believe me, is something else again.' The relish that infected Cockburn's voice when he spoke of large sums of money, was there again – a mixture of schoolboy wonder and greed. 'She calls herself an actress. She is, was a friend, perhaps rather a close friend, of Nini Montiam, but I gather they see less of each other now. Argentinian. And close for a time to the Perón household in Madrid. About thirty years old. Perhaps a touch more. Anyway she was around a great deal during all the negotiations and I got to know her very well. Very well indeed. Expensive of course. She expected presents. But. Well. My goodness.'

Roberto found it quite difficult to avoid showing his distaste for this, but he managed.

'Anyway, a month ago she rang me up in London. A second lot of tapes has turned up. Far hotter, far more sensational than the first lot, and it's darling Pepita who has them. She has them in a vault of the Banco de la Victoria de los Angeles, in Velázquez, and she wants me to hear them. Tomorrow at one o'clock. And I want you to come along and hear them with me.'

'Why?'

'You are an expert on Perón. I've made enquiries. You are the best Perón expert in Madrid. Coffee, I think. And what do you say to a brandy?'

Roberto waited while the table was cleared, brandy and coffee served. Then slowly he shook his head.

'They must be forgeries, Mr Cockburn. I am sure they must be. Someone has set you up. You are about to be the victim of a hoax. What do you call it? A con. From the French?'

'No. From confidence trick. I don't see how you can say all that. I don't see why you should. Sight unseen. You haven't heard the evidence. You're prejudging the case.' Cockburn was no longer Mephistophelean or coy. More a spoilt boy told after all to lay off the candy.

'But it stinks of it.' Roberto was emphatic. 'You've burnt your fingers once. Spent time and money on a wild goose hunt. You want to recoup your losses, regain your lost face. You're ripe to be the mark. And this González woman knows it.'

Cockburn's face flushed. Roberto sensed he was not only a spoilt boy, but a spoilt boy with a temper.

'So you won't do it?'

'Do what?'

'Come tomorrow to hear these tapes. Authenticate them.'

'Oh, I'll come. It will be an interesting experience. Oh yes, I'll come. But Mr Cockburn?'

'Steve.'

'As you wish. Steve. I must ask you this. Do you want me to give my real opinion of these tapes, once I've heard them? Or merely authenticate them? I mean, quite clearly, what you want is to have them authenticated.'

'I'm sorry. I don't quite see the... Yes, I do. See the difference, I mean. I don't suppose you intend to be impertinent. But I am quite serious about this. I want your honest professional opinion. That is all. And I shall pay a fee. A professional consultancy fee. Would a hundred dollars be about right?'

'No fee, Mr Cockburn, Steve. No fee. Well. I'll take ten dollars as a symbol, as a sign that we are keeping the matter on a business footing. All right?'

'Fine. And do please try to come tomorrow with an open mind.'

'Of course. You can count on that. I shall be entirely unprejudiced. I shall assess these tapes on grounds of sound, voice, speech mannerisms, and so forth, and of course, too, on grounds of content. And you shall have my absolutely professional, unprejudiced, and candid opinion. Roberto's smile was open, jolly. 'What a very pleasant meal it has been.' His glasses twinkled in the candlelight. 'And so interesting too.' He raised his globe of brandy, savoured the fumes that came off it. Not often did he drink really good Spanish brandy, made in Jérez with as much care as the best of sherries.

6

STOP.

'Is that right? Have I got it right? Done justice to myself and to the facts as far as possible? I think so. That damned gun. That *damned* gun. If I had not taken that gun would Ramón have been able to defend himself? *¿Quién sabe? No sé.* I don't know. Doesn't bear thinking about. Mustn't think about it. Must get on. Time? Ten o'clock. Near enough. What next? That first visit to the vault of the Banco de la Victoria de los Angeles, just off Velázquez in Recoletos. That was an amusing occasion in many ways. And one which . . . I can simply tell exactly as it happened. As indeed is the case so far.'

PLAY AND RECORD:

'So. Next day, after a late breakfast – after such a large meal I had not slept well – I set off to meet Steve Cockburn at the place and at the time appointed.'

STOP.

'I'm cold. Very cold. But not as cold as the Caudillo. Ha! Where's the electric fire . . . Oh Jesus.'

'I took the Metro from José Antonio, changed at Alonso Martínez...'

The Recoletos branch of the Victory of the Angels Bank was comfortable. Very comfortable. It resembled the lounge or cocktail bar of a very expensive, very modern, very chic hotel. Dotted like islands in a dark green sea of deep pile carpet, heavy black glass tables stood on satin steel legs with deep leather chairs that soughed when you sat in them. A curved counter with a rounded satin steel edge was also upholstered with black leather, of just the right resistance to make writing cheques or deposit slips a pleasure, not a chore; it swept round two sides and took the place of the bar one expected. Only the *caja*, the *caisse*, gave the show away – a toughened glass cage enclosed the cashier – a man with satin steel hair in a midnight-blue suit, who looked more like a prosperous brain surgeon than a teller.

There were not many customers. Three or four ladies dressed in black but with discreet touches of colour here and there, and hair blown into pastel confections, sat at one of the tables. The bank had even provided them with coffee. They gossiped intimately, faces very close, claw-like hands jangling with chains and jewels, gesturing neatly, sharply, in time to their hard, clipped Madrileño consonants and flattened vowels.

Roberto sat in a corner near the door and waited. He was very conscious of the tiny shabbinesses in his clothes, cursed Cockburn for being late, wondered how long it would be before one of the flunkies asked him his business, asked him to leave. Hardly though, he thought to himself, will they take me for a Basque bank robber.

Then through the tinted glass of the door he saw Cockburn's backside as he stooped to pay off a taxi. The tall Englishman strode in as if he were a shareholder, glanced round, found Roberto in his corner. He wore the same suit

33

as the night before but with matching waistcoat this time, beneath a short, dark, velvet-collared topcoat that he had left unbuttoned. Very English.

'Pepa González not here yet?'

Roberto bit back the negative that flew to his lips, glanced around and shrugged.

Cockburn took in the company and half-smiled. 'No. None of those is Pepita.' He took a red and gold cigarette pack from his pocket, lit the Dunhill with a gold lighter. 'You don't, do you?'

Roberto touched his chest in polite refusal.

'Well. I wonder what we'll hear. What she'll choose to play us. Listen. I hope you don't mind my saying this. But play it a bit close, won't you. I mean, don't let on in front of Pepa what your opinion is.'

Roberto gave the tiniest of shrugs.

Then there she was. Dark red hair shot with gold, eye-shadow and rouge reddish brown, green eyes, a long straight black sable, black court shoes. A single strand of large pearls glowed round her very white neck and a diamond winked on one finger. She was beautiful with that exact beauty that beautiful women discover in their thirties – not the ripe allure of adolescence, nor the thin grandeur some older women achieve – but that perfection that says that nothing of importance has been lost since the first glamour descended, and much has been learnt.

'*Pepita querida*,' breathed Cockburn, kissed first her fingers, then her cheek. Roberto hung back and took in, as Cockburn had not, the presence of a man and a woman behind her. The man was fortyish, perhaps more, not tall, no taller than Señora González in her high heels, but solidly built. He was well-groomed, had sandy hair, a little whitened, brushed thinly over a large round head, strong hands, small feet. He wore a coat that was camel-coloured but made from something more expensive. His small eyes were alert and wary, feral. Roberto did not much like the look of him, but was aware that ancient prejudices were at work. Especially he did not like the way his bearing towards Señora González subtly expressed ownership. Although not obvious it reeked of machismo, the arrogance of the Latin American with the woman he uses as his mistress.

The woman behind him was more interesting. Dressed in a plain brown tailored suit she was tall with very short white blonde hair. At first glance she could have been as young as Pepita, but then one realised she was much older, perhaps fifteen years older. Her face was lined, wrinkled even, and her fingers long and thin – most extraordinary was the colour of her skin which was very brown, but sun brown not racially brown.

'Steve, I must introduce you to my friend. Enrico Gunter. Enrico is also a businessman and will advise me on the business side of it all. And Becky Herzer you already know of course.'

Cockburn was clearly shocked by the presence of the tall middle-aged lady, and barely acknowledged Gunter.

'Becky. Damn it. What the hell are you doing here?'

Herzer smiled. 'Ever the dashing charmer. Much the same as you, I suppose.'

'Listen, I hope this doesn't mean an auction situation. I mean, damn it, we were on the same side last time.'

'And can be again this time. We must talk about it.' She had an accent, not a real one, a Berlitz one, just a hint of something American over carefully Europeanised vowels.

González indicated Roberto. 'And this is your expert?'

'Roberto Constanza y Fairrie.'

'Ah. I think I know the name. You are, like me, a Porteño, yes? From Buenos Aires.'

Roberto bowed acquiescence.

'And you are an expert on *El Conductor, El Lider*?'

'Yes.'

'Not as expert as I. I knew him. Rather well.' She clicked a finger at one of the clerks behind the counter. '*Oiga. El director y ahora.*'

This was rude and the old ladies stopped their sibilant clatter, looked up. Djinn-like the manager appeared. He was a tall, cadaverous man with eyes deep-set in sockets of mauve tissue. Long fingers and wrists flopping from the cuffs of a light grey suit welcomed them, gestured them through a gap in the bar that had miraculously swivelled open. Buttons were pressed, plastic cards threaded through electronic devices and a section of wall, also upholstered in leather, sighed open. The manager, González, Cockburn, Gunter, Herzer and Roberto descended steps beneath a small chandelier set beyond the opening.

The ambience remained much the same. The carpeted stairs led to another upholstered door that also whispered open obedient to the sesame of finger-tapped buttons. Beyond was a square room, quite large, with chairs and tables the same as those above. Three walls were lined to shoulder height with lockers much like those one finds at railway stations, but finished in satin steel. Above them on the wall facing the door and filling almost all of it was an enormous canvas. In blues set against browns, muted reds, greens, or lightning lit so they appeared to flash, twisting in perfect parabolas of flight and energy, a hundred handsome good angels put to flight a hundred handsome not so good angels, banished them to Erebus. San Miguel reported back to God's Mother who signalled her approval.

Roberto almost fainted at the wonder of it. '*La Victoria de los Angeles*,' he murmured. '*De Jacopo Robusti Tintoretto*. The Devil!'

No one else there seemed much bothered.

Señora González walked to a locker beneath the painting, fed a card into a slot. The manager handed her a small key, the door, far thicker than one finds on railway stations, swung open.

Cockburn's gold lighter rasped again. The cadaverous manager was politely terrified. '*Señor, no fumar, por favor!*'

'What? Oh, sorry.'

Gunter pulled a Philips tape-recorder from the locker, and then a smaller cassette player. In the space at the back Roberto could see a stack of cased spools and cassettes. Gunter released a flex and fitted it into a power point. González selected a cassette, uncased it, and handed it to Gunter who slotted it in. She looked up at the manager.

'*Déjenos, señor.*'

Reluctantly he went.

'*Sientense, por favor.*'

Gunter sat back, ankles crossed, hands clasped on his stomach. Cockburn was less relaxed, propped his head on one palm and with the other hand pushed fingers down on his unlit cigarette, reversed it, repeated the movement for as long as the tape played. Herzer sat next to him, knees together, back straight but leaning forward slightly, head on one side. She really was very thin, very brown, and very fit for her age. Roberto felt a tiny stir of desire which rather surprised him. He polished his glasses.

González kept the player on her knee, one finger resting on the stop button.

'What you are about to hear,' she said, 'was recorded by Don Juan Perón, at his weekend residence in Olivos, a suburb of Buenos Aires, some time after he was re-elected President of Argentina in October '73, just over two years ago.'

She pressed the play button. Tape hissed. Then a click, a tiny cough. The voice was quiet, confidential, a little throaty, fluent, at ease with itself.

7

'Don Martín, Ricardo Bauer, he likes to be called, but for me he will always be Don Martín, came over from San Isidro this afternoon. His first personal call. I teased him about his *estancia* there. El Brujo has told me about it. Fortified. Barbed wire. German shepherd dogs, the lot. Why bother, Don Martín, I asked him. I'm back. You have nothing to fear in Argentina now I am back. "It's to be like the old days again, then, is it, Don Juan?" Yes, I told him, like the old days.

'Poor man. He has aged. Aged a lot. And of course he's five years younger than me, but I swear he looks ten years older. He's lost weight. His eyes have that old look... senility. He is as old as this tired old century, I, five years older than that. But I think I've weathered our difficult times better than Don Martín.

'We reminisced. The old times...

'El Brujo tells me Don Martín went to Dr Ciacaglini, the rejuvenation expert. Because he has a new girlfriend. Perhaps he'll bring her too next time. Anyway. He can't get it up for her. So he went for the monkey gland bit. Ha! Hah, ha! Always there has been something, what's the word? *simian* about Don Martín.

'We reminisced. Old hands. Good times. He always hit it off with Evita. With Evita... he got on well.

'I must say, in some respects, I found him... over-bearing. Pompous. In the past. And now, he is a bit of a bore, the way old men are. He expects me to be grateful. For what? That a little of the millions he and Eva put on one side was spent on keeping me and Isabelita comfortable, tolerably comfortable, during my years of exile? Come on, Don Martín, I said, you know it is not as simple as that. He shrugged, conceded. Martín and I are a mutual protection society. He sometimes forgets this: I, never.

'Of course it was not only Don Martín. There were... thirty thousand?

'They came to Argentina. That is well-known. We welcomed them. Why not? They brought with them much that would help the development of the organic society that it has ever been my wish to create. Industrial know-how. Wealth. Technological advances were possible because of their presence, though not as many as one might have expected. The real brains were siphoned off through us to Uncle Sam.

'Many of them have done much for the growth of our cultural traditions, particularly in the sphere of music. As they have become part of our organic society and married into some of our best families, they have added a useful strain to what is already a valuably heterogeneous gene pool. I am indebted to the writer Robert Ardrey for this perception. One can see this brought to fruition in the performance of our boxers, tennis players, scientists and so on, with each succeeding generation.

'So. I have no regrets about this. Nothing to be ashamed of. After all, Don Martín never personally killed a man, woman, or child. I have his personal word for this fact. Not even a Jew. Of course, he signed papers. But if that is murder then all rulers are guilty. No one rules without signing pieces of paper.

'Anyway, crusty old fool that he now is, with his

new girlfriend, a Chilean I understand and only in her forties, I welcome him. He is someone from the past. An old friend. Someone who knew Evita. The real Evita.

'And certainly, it's true, where would either of us have ever got without Don Martín?'

CLICK.

8

Five seconds of silence, then Cockburn murmured: 'Don Martín?'

Herzer recrossed her long legs and looked up – puzzled at his uncertainty, then very definite. 'Bormann. Of course. Martin Bormann.'

Cockburn hissed: 'Shit.'

All shifted in their chairs and the leather creaked and soughed again. Cockburn shrugged and with a Byronic determination to do as he liked put his cigarette in his mouth. Herzer, very quickly, twisted her thin body towards him and snapped a tiny lighter cased in tortoiseshell. Cockburn inhaled, breathed out, an alarm bell rang, and rain began to fall. It increased in intensity. Gunter made for the door but it had bolted itself. The rain became steady, needle-sharp, and inescapable. A steel screen dropped over the *Victory of the Angels*. Everyone, except Roberto was suddenly rather angry. The skins of furry animals may have been waterproof for them, but Señora González was not entirely sure they would not be ruined on her. Cockburn dropped his cigarette near Roberto, who picked it up, sodden and dead as it was, and put it back on the carpet near where Cockburn had been sitting. Herzer unplugged the still live recorder, picked it up and carried it towards González, but caught her shin on the corner of the glass-topped table. She dropped the recorder. Gunter helped her to retrieve it, and the spilled cassette. They handed both to González. With backs pressed against the walls they waited for the downpour to cease. Pockmarked puddles began to form in the carpet.

At last it stopped. The door clicked open. The cadaverous manager, as minatory as Tintoretto's St Michael, stood on the threshold.

'There is a fixed charge for the offence committed,' he said, 'regardless of the damage caused, which may well exceed the indemnity. Five hundred thousand pesetas. I will respect a note of hand to that sum before I release you.'

Cockburn was angry.

'*Après vous le déluge*,' murmured Herzer. Roberto remembered it was the tall Czech girl who had lit Cockburn's cigarette and he thought Cockburn might hit her.

Wet though they were they went briefly to Pepa's apartment which was nearby. It was furnished in that brand of bourgeois good taste Roberto most hated. The curtains were velvet, the clock on the wall was a gilt sunburst, the carpet was apple green, white and pink with a raised pattern of flowers, the furniture was upholstered in cream hide, on the walls were very competently painted views of the Spanish Pyrenees done in exaggeratedly bright colours – violet, red, emerald, orange. There were no books, not even a leather-bound set of Baroja. But there was a very new Akai music centre – gleaming matt steel finish, stereo radio, double tape decks, record player, the lot, but only six records as far as Roberto could see. Julio Iglesias, Jacques Brel, flamenco, James Last, Argentinian tango. He shuddered. A maid, an old woman dressed in black, brought them coffee and brandy.

'Well,' asked Cockburn, 'what do you think?'

Roberto took off his spectacles, polished them, put them back on. It was important, he knew, to get the next bit exactly right. He was careful not to look at Señora González.

'Not too much.'

'Eh?'

'I don't like it. Frankly I don't think it's Perón.'

'On what grounds?'

'It's very difficult to say. I should like to hear more.'

'Wouldn't we all!'

'I need to spend some time on analysis. At the moment it's mainly a question of feel. It just doesn't feel quite right to me.'

Cockburn turned to González who had been listening to this with a very slight smile flickering round her lips. It made her more enchanting than ever.

'I must say, Pepa, it didn't sound quite the same as the other tapes.'

She offered the tiniest of pouts, a hint of a shrug. 'These are later. The cassettes at any rate. Done not long before he died. He was ten years older and a sick man. And then, too, they were done on equipment which was both more modern and yet in some ways not so good. On a modern, portable cassette machine. Of course they sound different.'

Enrico intervened: 'There is of course no need for us to get into an argument about this. I'm sure Mr Cockburn understands that he is not the only interested buyer. If he chooses to believe that what he has heard is some sort of forgery then that is his affair.'

Cockburn looked bewildered, even angry. He turned back to Roberto. 'Let's get this straight. You are talking about feel, hunch. You have not one single specific reason for supposing that what we heard is not Perón.'

Roberto thought for a moment, then pulled at his nose between thumb and finger. 'You could say that.'

'Will you stand by that?'

'On what I've heard so far, I'll stand by that.'

Cockburn insisted: 'There is no reason for supposing that what we heard is a forgery?'

'No.'

Herzer intervened: 'Fine, fine. But there is another

factor, that I really do think should be cleared up.'

'What?'

She pulled her tweed skirt over her brown knee. She was suddenly very intent, as if the question was a matter of great importance to her. 'Provenance. Where did these tapes come from? How did Pepa González come by them? Can she show title?'

They all, Enrico Gunter included, looked at González.

She dabbed a cigarette out in a cream-coloured marble ashtray.

'That,' she said, 'is something I will not disclose at the moment. When an offer has been made, a cheque signed, then I will reveal both how these tapes came to be in Madrid, and why I am entitled to dispose of them.'

'Right.' Cockburn was brisk now. 'I've heard enough to convince me I should contact Peter Clemann again. If he is as interested as I think he will be, I'm sure he'll fly out directly. Of course he'll want to hear plenty of the tapes himself. And I've no doubt he'll want Roberto here to continue checking them out. You'll be able to arrange that, Pepa?'

'Of course. If you promise not to smoke in the bank vault.'

'I promise.' He turned to Herzer. 'I really do think we should work together on this.'

'Oh yes. So do I, Steve. That is why I am here.'

'Quite. I can promise you I would have been in touch today, just as I will be with Peter. I had no intention of cutting you out.'

'Oh quite. Mind you, I must say this. I think you are unduly excited about the Bormann connection.'

'Really?'

'Really!' Her smile was conciliatory, that of a mother to a child whom she is about to disappoint. 'I think almost everything anyone could want to know about Bormann was on the Sassen tapes.'

'The what?'

44

'Come on, Steve. The tapes Eichmann recorded for a journalist called Sassen. Not long before he was kidnapped. Eichmann hated Bormann, you know? He said it all.'

'But that was ten years ago. This is virtually yesterday.'

Somewhere in the room a fly kept wakeful by central heating buzzed. Roberto was aware of silence, that Señora González was looking intently at Madame Herzer, intently but without expression. He wondered why.

González intervened, quite sharply: 'This is irrelevant. We are not concerned with these... what do you call them? Sassen tapes. I have for sale tapes made by Perón himself. Some made not long before he died. Why bother with Eichmann and Sassen when you can hear from Perón's own lips what Bormann personally said to him, and some of it less than eighteen months ago?'

Herzer looked at her. 'Very well.' Her tone was entirely equable. She turned back to Cockburn. 'Anyway, Steve, I think we should work out just how we are to work together.' She maintained a coolly humorous tone, which again Roberto found appealing.

Cockburn blundered on: 'Well. Shall we have dinner tonight?'

'If it's somewhere reasonable and you are paying.'

'El Botín?'

The best. Better than El Cid, thought Roberto.

'All right.'

'Half nine. You are in your studio flat? I'll call for you. I shall have heard from Peter by then.'

In the lift going down Cockburn said to Roberto: 'You know, old chap, I think you went a wee bit over the top, knocking that tape. It was pretty sensational stuff.'

'I gave my considered opinion. As I said I would. I was not swayed one way or another by what you said either last night or this morning.'

'But still no real reason for saying it's not Perón.'

'No real reason. But those tapes need to be analysed. Scientifically.'

'Well. We'll get to that once we've pushed on a bit with the deal. By the way. On that tape. The ... voice mentioned someone called El Brujo. The Wizard. The Warlock. Who he?'

'Nickname for José López Rega.'

'And?'

'Member of the Perón household.'

9

On the way back Roberto felt mildly depressed. His clothes, in spite of the ancient topcoat, still felt damp; the streets, in spite of continuing bright sunshine, struck cold, and the Metro was draughty. He feared sciatica more than anything. *Viva El Rey* sprayed everywhere. Why? Juan Carlos had shown no particular ability or strength of character. For years he had been a puppet, an appendage, standing behind the Caudillo at army parades, tall, slightly absurd, not unlike that English comedian with the same initials... John Cleese, was that it?... who, like Juan Carlos, did funny walks. Perhaps the graffiti writers meant Don Juan, the prince's father, and the rightful ruler. What a mess it was all going to be.

There were frightful stories about Franco. Ramón heard them in the cafés he frequented. How below the thorax gangrene had set in. How the people who monitored the machines that kept the cadaver clinically alive could scarcely bear the stink. And when they finally switched him off what then? It wasn't even certain the royal princes wouldn't compete for the crown, father against son, the Spanish disease.

And the same now in Argentina. Isabelita, Perón's third wife, would not last in power much longer. A few months at the most. Then what? A Pinochet or worse. Civil war with a Pinochet at the end of it. No doubt who would win. The United States would see to that.

The anxiety was twisted further towards fear when he changed at Alonso Martínez. The Chilean assassin was a hero not only in Argentina – he had his followers in Madrid too. A young man wearing a long leather coat aerosoled the walls of the tiled tunnel between platforms: *Del Bosch – Nuestra Pinochet*. Two soldiers and a businessman stood by and watched with approval. Others, including Roberto, hurried on down the echoing passage, eyes averted, pretending not to have noticed. General Milans del Bosch fought for Hitler on the Russian Front with the Blue Division – the swastika with which the youth completed his artwork lay well alongside his name.

Roberto struggled up the steps at the José Antonio Metro, and then up the four flights of stairs past the *pensión* in Desengaño. The unillusioned one. The one who knows it all and doesn't like it.

Ramón was in the kitchen burning a potato omelette. Taller, thinner, about fifteen years younger than Roberto, but a good friend, a very good friend.

'How did it go then?'

'All right. Much as I expected. But there was one very funny moment... ' He went on to describe how Cockburn's cigarette had set off the sprinklers.

Ramón unfastened most of the omelette from the bottom of the pan, cut it in half, poured cheap red wine from a starred litre bottle into two tall Duralex glasses. They sat, knees almost touching, at either side of the tiny kitchen table.

'I should tell you. Juan "Evita" has been hearing things.'

'What things?'

'That some very nasty characters know about these tapes. And they don't like what they know about them... '

Roberto remembered. Martin Bormann is alive and lives in... San Isidro. A posh resort up the Plate from Buenos Aires.

48

'Where did he hear that?'

'Come on. You know Juan. He leads a double life. For a lot of people he's a well-to-do, right-wing student from Buenos Aires, doing medical research on pain thresholds at Madrid University. OK?'

'All right.' Roberto pulled a lump of bread off the small French-shaped loaf they shared and pushed it round his chipped plate. 'Ask him what he can find out about Enrico Gunter.'

'Who's he?'

'I don't know. That's the point of asking "Evita" to ask around about him, isn't it?'

'Come on, Roberto. Don't be grumpy. Who is Enrico Gunter?'

'A smooth character who hangs around Señora Josefina González. An Argentinian. A businessman. And he claims he is offering her business advice on how to sell the tapes.'

Ramón agreed that Enrico Gunter needed looking into.

Roberto sneezed. 'I told you I got wet. Can I have the fire this afternoon?'

'Of course.'

They collected up the plates, washed up ineffectually, made coffee. Ramón smoked and Roberto, who had been a non-smoker for less than two years, envied him.

STOP.

But though Roberto's tape ceased to turn his voice went on.

'The fire. I cannot go to the bathroom. I cannot face that in the bathroom. But I'm cold, very cold. Eight, nine, ten, eleven o'clock. I don't suppose I could get the fire to work anyway. Probably kill myself trying to. May not be a bad thing. I did not kill Ramón. Not actually kill him. But oh, dear Lord, he'd surely be alive now if I'd never met him.

'If I can't keep warm I'll die anyway. No snow outside. And he's still there, or another very like him. He'll be even colder than I am. There'll be fog at sunrise. Freezing fog. I should have a hot drink. That's it.

'What's that noise? A rattling engine with a squeak, a squeal. Dear Lord, of course! Tanks. Tanks in the streets.'

He shuddered deeply. He'd seen tanks in the streets before. And dead bodies.

'Swearing in tomorrow. The new king. He'll make a speech to the Cortes. Are the tanks on his side? Probably they'll make up their minds when they've heard the speech. Tanks in Gran Vía. Round Cibeles, Sol, and Canovas. Blocking off the Cortes.

'Coffee or tea. Tea would be better. But you can't put brandy in tea. Any more coffee though will make me want to shit. And there are some things you cannot do in a kitchen sink. I cannot face the bathroom. I will not face the bathroom. Lipton's tea-bags. Such thin stuff. Infusions for ailing Spanish ladies. Friend used once to send me Jackson's Breakfast. Jackson's of Piccadilly. Two bags to one cup. And if I can't drink brandy with it, I can have some before. Could always put hot water in it. Should have thought of that. But not the bathroom.

'It's a funny thing about dead bodies. Some people can't see it. I suppose most who have been going to see that gangrenous cadaver in the Palace can't see it. What they can't see is that it's just meat. Putrid meat. The man has gone. An empty house. No, that's not it. Sentimental image. A house is a house. But a cadaver is not a man. The change is swift, in the twinkling of an eye, and no matter how slow or sudden the movement towards that moment, the moment itself is complete, final. Yes, you are. No, you are not.

'So that's not Ramón in there, and that's why it is so hateful. If it were Ramón I could do something for him.

50

'Brandy first. Then tea. Then back to the tape. Something I owe Ramón. Something I can do for the real Ramón, not the obscenity in the bath...'

10

'I met Ramón Puig quite by chance in the Prado. It was autumn, just over a year ago. When I come back to Madrid I go, as soon as I can, to the Prado, to meet again old friends. Charles the Fourth and his family. Those peasants pushing their way through a blizzard with a pig. Poor pig. La Maja with and without her clothes.

'Cockburn goes straight to a restaurant and has a *torre de mariscos*. I go to the Prado and meet old friends again. Always I leave to last the best. I expect Cockburn leaves the largest crayfish to the end as well. Sometimes in the summer there is a queue. Japanese. Arabs even. In September it's not so bad. Just five or six people – serious people who know why they are there.

'It... you cannot say *it*. They – the dwarfs, the princess, Diego himself, and that magical figure in the lit doorway – have a little room to themselves. Often the leaded window is open; there is quite a fuss on at the moment about the way the Prado is run, and no doubt it will be improved. But September a year ago, with bright sunshine, the leaded window was open, and I liked that. It put the painting in the context of our lives, made it a real thing. Paintings are no more immortal than we are. Traffic fumes spoil their health, may kill them in the end, just as they do us. So what? With reasonable care they still live a lot longer than we. And reasonable care means letting them live as part of our lives, live and die with us – not shut off in artificial climates behind glass that inevitably reflects.

'So. I liked the open window. There were other things I liked too. I liked the heavy, intricately carved black frame, and I liked the way they have put a mirror in an exactly similar frame opposite it. So you can stand and see the painting exactly framed but in a mirror image, and see the painting, and so on. I'm not quite sure why this works. Somehow it brings us into the world of the picture, we become the hidden people who are painted on the other side of Diego's canvas, Philip IV of Spain and Mariana of Austria, visited now by their daughter Margarita who wants to show off the finery her dwarfish maids have put her in. For surely she looks at them, at her parents (at us), as if at a mirror, to see from their reaction the truth of how she really is...

'I like also the small marble plaque which says: *Las Meninas de Diego Rodríguez de Silva y Velázquez... La última obra del Arte.*

'I like it because it tells the truth.

'And on that warm September day, with touches of gold in the chestnuts outside, I became conscious that the man next to me was quietly tearful too at the perfection of the greatest painting of all time...'

Roberto murmured: 'A fino perhaps?'

The stranger, taller, thinner, ten or fifteen years younger, with a black and grey beard very close-cropped so it was little more than stubble, dressed in a loosely-knit dark blue sweater, spotless jeans and blue canvas shoes, muttered assent: 'Why not?'

In a way they were like lovers, instantly aware of over-powering Eros, but knowing nothing of each other, having to explore and discover each other's personality. Except that with Roberto and Ramón the attraction had nothing to do with sex, or at any rate not in the way the word is usually understood, but rather with an equally powerful and sudden sense that they shared a similar sensibility. And the voyage of discovery into each other's life was instantly fraught with embarrassment – both were impossibly poor and, while neither was proud, neither wanted to admit it: for if one turned out to be well-to-do, then the other would be cast, would cast himself, in the role of sponger, hanger-on.

So they went to the café on the other side of the Paseo, just below the Banco de España, where they sat in chairs upholstered in plastic wicker-work, beneath elaborate awnings, surrounded by potted bays, and with a spotless white table-cloth in front of them. They drank two dry sherries each and ate a handful of pistachios, and when they shared the bill they discovered that each had blown the food and drink budget for a whole day.

Ramón Puig had a sallow face, lined, with deep-set dark eyes, long brown fingers with white nails which flickered ceaselessly in tiny gestures as he spoke.

They talked about Velázquez and Goya without pretension, but with shared enthusiasm. Later they discovered similar shared obsessions with Mozart, the *esperpento* theatre of Spain, Fred Engels, Buenos Aires, Barcelona, and lost causes.

Ramón Puig's father had been a Catalan actor who had devoted the early part of his life to trying to establish a national Catalan theatre. His sister, Ramón's aunt, had married an Argentinian businessman of Catalan descent whom Roberto vaguely remembered as being a distant connection of his own wife, from whom he had been separated since 1945. At the end of the Spanish Civil War, therefore, Ramón's father had been able to take his family into exile to Buenos Aires. There Ramón, himself, made his début as an actor, as an extra, in a cut version of *Luces de Bohemia* by Valle-Inclán. This was in 1953, the very year Roberto began his wanderings.

54

When they had finished their finos they walked up the sidestreets near the Cortes, crossed Alcalá, and so came to Desengaño where they spent the rest of the day listening to Mozart on tapes. Ramón invited Roberto to become co-tenant, and Roberto accepted. They lived discretely, minded each other's business, but often shared long meals with little to eat but plenty of cheap red wine, through the afternoons in the tiny kitchen.

On his second day there Roberto asked what was the history of the street's name.

'Calle del Desengaño.' Ramón stubbed out and shredded the dark tobacco of his cigarette, drank more *tinto*. '1650s. Thereabouts. Two *caballeros* in love with the same woman, set off down the street, don't know what it was called then, to fight a duel.' His thin fingers flickered like rapiers. 'A dark shadow passed between them, a cloaked figure.' His hand, flat and vertical, floated across the table. 'A woman? Their woman? Perhaps. They followed. Came to the corner. The figure turned ... ' – Ramón's eyes went large, the white of them glowed in the gathering shadows of the kitchen, his jaw dropped – simultaneously he was a death's head and the astonishment of the gallants – ' ... a *memento mori* – a skull with dried skin, rotten teeth, and ... ' – his little finger rose up, writhed like a tiny snake – ' ... worms in her eyes!' His face took on an expression of lofty disdain. 'There was a stink of putrefaction. "*Qué desengaño*," exclaimed one of the gallants, and arm in arm, off they went to the nearest tavern.' He drank his wine, poured more for both of them, saluted Roberto. 'Friends after all ... '

Desengaño.

'Not a word for which there is an exact English equivalent. The awakening, the awakened, the breaking of the spell, the unenchanted and so the disenchanted, the unillusioned.'

STOP.

Then PLAY AND RECORD:

'There was no further awakening for me with Ramón. No disenchantment. We did not get to know each other any better after those first few days. We did not need to.'

11

'I awoke the next morning, that is the first morning after the first hearing of the dictator's tapes, in something of a quandary. Cockburn knew my address and I knew his. But since those who live in the street of the unenchanted have no telephones, well not in the despised *ático* apartments, there was no ready way he could make contact with me. I was reluctant that he should call and discover the rather reduced circumstances in which I live. Naïve people, and I rather suppose Cockburn to be naïve, tend to believe expertise is demonstrated by the trappings of success. The history of medicine alone proves him wrong – the greater the quackery, the greater the rewards.

'He had been to dinner – and possibly to bed – with Señora Becky Herzer. Or perhaps after dinner with Herzer he had returned to Recoletos and bed with González. I did not expect him to be awake early. I therefore telephoned – from one of the public call boxes outside the José Antonio Metro station – a message to the Príncipe Hotel that if he wanted to contact me during the day a message could be left at the Biblioteca Nacional.

'The Spanish National Library is not the most efficient institution in the world, but I felt an investment of a hundred pesetas in the cream marbled hall, which is the last of the many barriers that keep books and people apart, would pay reasonable dividends. I came back to it roughly on the hour throughout the day – tearing myself away from Marañón's biography of Antonio Pérez, the favourite of Philip II – and found a message waiting for me at 2 p.m.

'It was terribly garbled of course, quite unintelligible – Cockburn's unsatisfactory Spanish and the stupidity, or at any rate lack of interest (really one hundred pesetas was not enough) of the clerk who had taken the call made sure of that.

'I rang the Príncipe. Cockburn passed on the necessary information. Clemann and he, and, he hoped, I too, would be at the bank the following morning at eleven o'clock. With us would be Professor James McCabe of Milton University, Iowa – an expert on Perón and Argentina, known as such throughout the world. Professor McCabe would help me to authenticate or discredit the tapes.

'Known throughout the world? Not to me. I went back into the Biblioteca to find out what I could about McCabe.

'The following morning I took the Metro again to Velázquez – tedious journey since it involves a change and takes one across two sides of a triangle – and found myself, after Alonso Martínez, looking through the connecting windows between two carriages at Clemann and Cockburn. I assumed it was Clemann and it turned out I was right.

'From the way his knees stuck up I realised he was very tall. He wore glasses framed heavily in black, a dark topcoat made from blue and black tweed, dark brown gloves, a striped suit. He looked like an English academic. Cockburn and he said little as the train swayed in and out of Colón and Serrano and I guessed Cockburn was annoyed, peeved, at going by public transport. Clemann clearly had a millionaire's view of the value of money and was not going to ignore the wisdom of the City Fathers of Madrid who have set a blanket single fare on the Metro of eight pesetas with reductions if you buy a book of tickets. I wondered if Clemann had invested in a book... it would indicate how long he expected to stay.

'At Velázquez I let them move on up ahead and hung back too as they walked round two sides of a block to the bank. Thus I became aware of a man with longish dark curly hair, swarthy skin, a black leather jacket and jeans, with two-tone black and white thick-soled shoes who was walking with me. And his actions too were directed by the two people in front of us. When Cockburn paused to light a cigarette on the corner we paused together to stare, side by side, into a shop window which displayed one silk oriental rug of majestic elegance priced at my current income for one year. Then we both hurried on to the corner round which they had gone.

'Well. "Evita" had told Ramón that news of the existence of this second lot of Perón tapes, if that is what they are, was talked of in fascist circles in Madrid. While my companion did not look like one of them, he certainly did have the appearance of the sort they employ as lackeys. I have every reason to fear that sort of person. A mob of them burnt my shop off Calle Florida in Buenos Aires and damn near burned me. Jew go home to Moscow, they shouted, and *Juden raus*, and the man who poured out the demagogic bullshit that set them off was that charlatan windbag who seems to have spent most of his later years talking to himself on tape.

'Anyway, not wishing to draw his attention to me I crossed the road to a kiosk, bought a copy of *Cambio 16* whose cover announced that the nation and the world were waiting for the termination of the Caudillo. The black-jacketed lout stayed on his side, only a shop front away from the bank, and he too lit a cigarette.

'Presently another tall man, unmistakably another Anglo-Saxon, came briskly up Velázquez, head and shoulders above everyone else in the street: he wore a pork-pie hat, had a yellowish complexion, a long nose, a short raincoat, brownish tweeds, carried a briefcase. Brisk, yes, and the way he sidestepped to avoid one of the elderly

59

ladies on the bank's steps and then lurched forward put me inescapably in mind of Jacques Tati. I soon learnt that this over-tall gaucheness was the only point of similarity. I took him, correctly, to be McCabe.

'I was in a quandary. The lout remained on watch, but I had seen everyone concerned arrive except González, Herzer, and Gunter, and they might already be inside. If they were then all might proceed to the vault without me. Therefore I dropped *Cambio 16* in a bin – I already had a copy at home – and crossed only to arrive on the step of the bank at exactly the same time as Señora González. She smiled most pleasantly at me as I held the door for her and I could not help noticing the exquisite fragrance of her perfume as I followed her in...

'The three tall men unfolded their legs almost like giraffes from the low chairs they must have only just sat in. Not like giraffes. More like herons or storks. For a moment I felt that Señora González and I were as vulnerable as fish in a pool...'

12

Cockburn introduced Clemann and McCabe to Roberto, and McCabe to González. Clemann was quiet, incisive, courteous. McCabe had thin gingery hair brushed artlessly to cover near baldness, gold-rimmed spectacles, mottled hands with loose skin and limp fingers.

'No Gunter then today, Pepa?' asked Cockburn. It was a crow, betraying that for him Gunter's absence was good news.

'No, Steve,' Señora González replied, 'Enrico has a business appointment he could not postpone. It's of no importance. He has already heard the tape I intend to play today and anyway, as I told you, he is to advise me on the actual terms of the sale, and I do not expect to make too much progress in that direction right now. Señora Herzer also phoned me. She too has an appointment she could not break but I gather your dinner date went well with her and she will work with you again.' Roberto thought: so Herzer was bedded by Cockburn who would rather have bedded González who was being bedded by Gunter. Then he shuddered at the multiple idiocy of this reflection and the inner confusions it revealed. 'Gentlemen, shall we go down? And this time, please, *no fumar*. All right?'

Again there was the rigmarole of opening the door to the vault and then that of Señora González's locker. She took out the cassette recorder at the front and then signalled Roberto to come forward and help her with the far larger and heavier spool-to-spool machine. He dragged it out, set it flat, discovered some difficulty in finding how the catches on the lid worked, and the hatch behind in which the flex was stored, but he managed it all to her instructions. She then handed him a six-centimetre spool and asked him to thread it up. He fumbled this and Cockburn, with brusque impertinence, intervened.

'Here, let me.'

Roberto stood aside.

Señora González, her eyebrows slightly raised, said: 'Set the counter to zero.'

Cockburn did so.

'Now wind forward until the counter reads 068.'

Certainly he was more adept with the machine than Roberto had been.

'Good. Now before I play this extract I think I should provide a little historical background. It will be familiar to Señor Fairrie and Professor McCabe if they are as expert in the life of *El Conductor* as they claim. But it could be useful for Mr Clemann.'

'I don't think that will be necessary,' said Clemann. 'I pay to have experts decide for me what I cannot decide for myself. If they understand the background of what we are about to hear, then there's no need for you to fill it in on my account.'

Señora González thought for a moment. Then: 'Nevertheless. What you are about to hear is sensational. It would not be believed by you for one moment even if your experts accepted it, unless you heard some of the background, the circumstances that make it credible.'

Clemann had manners as well as intelligence. With an odd movement of his head, not a shake or a nod but something between, he gave her the floor.

She took it with presence. She was dressed much as she had been before – the sable, which she now took off, the black dress. But this time, instead of the pearls she had a small emerald brooch above her left breast.

'You are,' she said, 'all more or less aware of the phenomenon known as Evita. The second wife of Juan Perón. Of how she came from humble origins – the details of which are still disputed – became an actress on the Argentinian radio, in Argentinian films. The mistress of Perón shortly before he became the Vice-President in the mid-forties...'

Indeed Roberto was familiar with all this. Momentarily he lost himself in contemplation of Tintoret's *Victory of the Angels*. It was lovely. Presumably belonged to the bank. Did the bank take its name from the painting? Or had the bank bought it because it already bore that name... the whim of a director? The St Michael especially was very fine – admittedly owing something to Michelangelo's Christ in the *Last Judgment*, but none the worse for that...

McCabe, however, did take an interest in what Señora González had to say. He leant forward over a small scribble pad held on his knee, and jotted notes with a gold-cased ball-point loosely held between white and orange fingers.

'What few people outside Argentina know much about,' Señora González was saying, 'and not many people in Argentina for that matter, is the nature of Evita's relationship with Juan Duarte, Juancito, her brother. He had few talents but was personable, even charming. From the moment Perón had patronage Evita assured Juancito's advance. He even became Perón's private secretary. He was basically a wastrel, a nonentity, a nobody. During the last years of his life, and Evita's, the dissipation that had always been an obsession became a habit. Several sources assert that he was syphilitic. Perón himself is on public record as to this, and there are people alive who claimed that Juancito admitted the disease to them.'

Somehow, from somewhere, she had arranged to have available a glass and a small bottle of Perrier. She poured and sipped.

'Nevertheless. Evita adored him, and did so from adolescence or earlier. While she was alive, he was indestructible. Once she was dead he was useless, an embarrassment. Just nine months after she died, on 6 April, 1953, he resigned his post as Perón's secretary. Three days later he was found dead, shot, in his apartment. He had taken off most of his clothes, which were folded neatly, and was in pants, vest and socks. He was on his knees by the bed, as if in prayer. There was a note, handwritten, that certainly reads like a suicide note, and contains the phrase: "I came with Eva, I leave with her."

'At that time he was being investigated by a commission of army officers who were inquiring into a meat shortage that had arisen because of speculation by government officials.'

Roberto remembered: a week later Perón incited the mob to burn . . . lots of things. Him. His shop. *El Conductor* had a lot of troubles just then. Fighting for his political life, as they say. But he damn near killed me as well.

González's voice went on: 'The joke everyone told at the time was "Everybody knows he committed suicide. Nobody knows who did it."'

Cockburn snickered. González again looked at him with slightly raised eyebrows. McCabe frowned, pulling sandy, almost invisible brows together. Clemann remained motionless as he had throughout, left ankle on his right knee, held by both hands, head a little on one side, alert. Señora González sipped Perrier again and the cunning light from above found spun gold in her hair and flashed fire from her emeralds. Roberto pushed the memory of the other fire to the back of his mind, and she went on.

'There is one more piece of this particular jigsaw to be fitted before I play the tape. It is still not certain, not publicly certain what Evita was suffering from, what killed her. Certainly for several years before her death she suffered increasing spasms of pain in the region of her groin and almost continual vaginal discharge. She was anaemic, so much so that leukaemia was spoken of. Her skin took on an unhealthy, coppery glow. She suffered almost continuously a low fever. In November '51 she at last consented to a hysterectomy, cancer of the womb having been suspected for some time. There is no public certainty that the operation discovered a malignant growth. Her condition continued to deteriorate until her death nine months later.

'Now I shall play the tape. It was recorded early in Perón's exile, perhaps even before he came to Madrid.'

13

All, even Clemann, shifted and the black leather creaked and sighed, but they froze as the voice, that voice came again. It sounded different. Of course this recording had been made at a quite different time, on an older machine, perhaps more like the one used on the tapes bought by *ABC* and Planeta. That, at any rate, was what they had been told. The tone of the voice was different too. Meditative, slow, with long gaps between phrases. One sensed that the speaker was close to the microphone, on his own, talking to himself at night, perhaps in the early hours of the morning.

'I know what they say. That I ordered the death of Juan Duarte Juan*cito*.' (The last two syllables came in something between a spit and a rasp.) 'Certainly I had good cause to. But my record... I stand by my record as a man of peace, a man who hates violence. Twice I have turned my back on my destiny to avoid inevitable and unnecessary bloodshed, and have been called a coward when the gratitude of thousands was my true desert. But Juan, Juan, Juancito.' (This time he drew out the whole word – starting with a guttural consonant, breathing the second syllable, and again spitting the *zeeto*, relishing his hate for it.) 'Yes. I had good reason to order his death. Those who say that are right, but little do they know how good the reason was. All right...' (The voice quickened a little.) '...he was a waster, a scoundrel, an idiot even. These are forgivable crimes. He was an incompetent. He botched all the work he ever did for Eva or for me – irritating, yes, but no reason for killing him. He abused his position, made money from it, a fortune... well, these are crimes – but not punishable by death. A good spell on Martín García, perhaps, but not the pistol to the head.'

At this point McCabe looked up, his glasses flashed. Then he scribbled busily, but briefly.

'But how about this. Suppose... suppose the First Lady's infatuation with this booby went beyond a purely sisterly affection...'

There was a long pause on the tape, the rasp of a lighter. Cockburn's hand too went to his pocket and froze there as González, basilisk-like, glared at him.

'It's been said,' (the voice went on – still meditative, still very much as if speaking to itself) 'it's been said Juancito and I had much... in common. Certainly Evita doted on him. As she did on me. Yes. He had charm. Looks. Anyway. Supposing his disease. Had been transmitted. In whatever ways such diseases are transmitted. To his sister. My wife. And she died of it. Then would I not have every reason in the world to order his death?'

CLICK.

They all stirred, coughed, sighed.
Clemann spoke. His voice was serious but polite, just coloured with a New England accent.
'Señora González, is that all we are to hear today?'
'Yes.'

'I doubt it's enough for our experts.' He turned enquiringly first to McCabe, then to Roberto.

McCabe flipped over the cover of his scribble pad, parked the gold ball-point. He cleared his throat.

'No, Clemann. Not enough.' His accent, a mid-West drawl, nasally delivered, was far more marked. 'No way can I make a sound judgment on what we have heard. An informed guess at best.'

'I have of course heard an earlier extract,' Roberto spoke, as Clemann turned to him, 'but there are very many questions to be asked. And answered.'

Cockburn could not restrain himself. 'But that was pretty sensational stuff. You must admit. I mean if that is real, if that is Perón, we have a very saleable commodity here. Damn it, it's worth a bomb.'

Roberto chewed his bottom lip, then: 'Perhaps, Mr Cockburn, your Spanish isn't quite up to the nuances, the tenses; he never actually says that Eva slept with her brother, that she died of syphilis, that he, Perón, killed Juancito. All the way it is conditional. If this, if that, then would I not...'

Cockburn's laugh was brusque. 'Come on. It's dynamite. You know it.'

'Come now,' Clemann intervened, 'it's not the saleability we're concerned with at the moment. It's the authenticity. How far are our experts prepared to go in that direction? Señor Fairrie, I gather you said of the first extract you heard that you had no reason to say that the voice was not Perón's. Do you still stand by that?'

'Yes. No. Yes.'

'You have reservations. I should like to know what they are.'

'I'm not happy about the voice. It's too... imitable. The genuine Perón, I mean. While I don't deny for one moment that it does sound very like him, I could not swear to it without scientific, electronic analysis.'

'But for that we would need not only the necessary

machinery and an expert to operate it, but an accredited sample of Perón's voice for comparison.'

'Yes.'

'And where will we find that?'

'*ABC*?' suggested González.

'Of course, *ABC* has one hundred and forty hours of accredited tape,' – Clemann's voice took on an edge, something stronger than mere ruefulness – 'but I doubt they'll let us borrow a sample so we can authenticate a set of tapes that will blow their product into limbo.'

'We can try,' said Cockburn.

'Sure. We can try.'

'And I don't think you need go to Geneva for an electronic voice analyser.' This was Roberto. 'Such equipment is in use in Madrid University. I have a friend who does not actually work with it, but his own line of research is related and he knows people who do.'

'Thank you. And what about you, Professor? What's your view?'

'Much the same as Señor Fairrie's. I have not heard enough to say definitely one way or the other. Not enough to assert categorically that it is not Perón. But . . . '

'You too have reservations.'

'Yes. But unlike Fairrie, I'm not too bothered about the voice. That can be tested, as he rightly says. It's the content bothers me.'

'The content?' Roberto's voice fluked up.

'Nothing specific. A feeling, not much more. As Cockburn says, it's dynamite. But dynamite to Peronismo. To the present government there which is toppling anyway, of course. But to the very survival of Peronismo after it's gone.'

'Why do you say that?'

'Look. Every conceivable slander, including this one, has been thrown at Evita from both the right and the left – and for the *decamisados* it just proves what shits they all are. But to hear something like this from the lips of *El Lider* himself... that would be pretty destabilising of the Evita image, which is central to modern day Peronismo.'

'Perhaps. But that doesn't necessarily cast doubts on the authenticity of this tape.'

'I think it does. Whatever Perón personally thought of the matter, he knew the absolute importance of the Evita myth. I just don't think he'd put something like that on tape.'

'What about Nixon? What about the White House tapes?' Cockburn again.

'Sure. That's a precedent. But,' – McCabe stroked his chin – 'whatever you think of Perón, he had something tricky Dicky just did not have. You could call it... class, I suppose.'

'Gentlemen. We're getting no further. Señora, you are adamant that you won't let us hear any more tape on this occasion?'

'Would there be any point? You want voice analysis. You set it up, and I may or may not allow it. I'll see.' She twisted the ring on her finger. 'But... I don't wish to be impertinent. But you have been in this market before. You lost out. There are many potential buyers, who may not be so choosy, so fussy as you.'

Clemann grimaced, unfolded himself from the low leather chair, moved towards the open locker. González followed him, placed herself just ahead of him.

'Four spools of tape. Thirteen cassettes. Not as much as *ABC* bought. The spools look the same sort of thing as they've got. Really, Señora González, I'm interested, I wouldn't be here if I was not. But that last trip cost me a lot – and before I spend any more money, I do need to know just a little bit more of what we are into.'

They faced each other. She barely came up to the top pocket of his jacket. She was aware of it, refused to look up at him, returned to her chair, sat forward on it, legs to the side and crossed at the ankles. She smoothed her skirt.

'The spools were done, we think, in Madrid during the

same period as those *ABC* bought. But Perón kept them separate from those precisely because he knew they contained very sensitive material. He had been more than usually indiscreet. They went back to Buenos Aires with him. In the baggage of one of his entourage. It's possible he thought they had been destroyed. Eight cassettes were made in the presence of the same companion during the months preceding Perón's death. He knew he was dying. Discretion was no longer important – only self-justification and an old man's desire to have some influence on history after his death. He was a vain man.'

Cockburn crowed: 'Surely that takes care of the Professor's quibbles about content?'

Clemann ignored him. 'And the other five cassettes?'

Roberto, confused, looked at Pepita with serious but expressionless eyes, and waited.

González looked at her immaculate fingernails, then, her eyes still cool, directly at Clemann.

'They are nothing to do with this. They are tapes I choose to keep here, but they were not made by Perón.'

Clemann nodded, apparently satisfied.

'All right. But you must realise that before we have a deal I must know where the Perón tapes came from, and what right you have to dispose of them.'

'I think you already know that I shall reveal that when a deal is struck. If then you don't like what I tell you, you will still be able to draw back.'

'And you want... ?'

'Two hundred thousand dollars – and you get the tapes to which I shall renounce all title.'

'A similar deal to the earlier one.'

González said nothing.

Clemann turned away, looked up into the *Victory of the Angels* for nearly two minutes. The others sat on, avoiding looking at each other for most of the time, though once, briefly, Cockburn's eyes met González's, and a ghost of a smile crossed both faces. Then Clemann turned back.

'Frankly, I don't like it. I'm not going into why right now. You can work it out for yourself. However, I've sent for a lawyer, Henry Swivel. I wish I'd had him here before. Becky Herzer – who somehow heard of all this already and felt she was entitled to get in on the act again is also around. They'll both be at El Príncipe Monday evening. Steve. You'll be there too. At the Príncipe, 7 p.m. We'll have a conference about it all and go on from there. Right?'

'Right.'

'Fairrie, McCabe. Thank you for your help so far. I can see difficulties about this voice analysis procedure, so I think it likely I'll need further help. I'd like you too, both of you, to be in Steve's room at the Príncipe at eight o'clock on Monday. I'm paying you expenses, that's right? And professional consultancy fees. Fairrie, Cockburn tells me you won't take more than ten dollars a throw. That's a gesture. You get a hundred every time I ask for you ... we do things properly or not at all.'

He turned back to González.

'Thank you, Señora. I appreciate your impatience with me, but today is Saturday, the bank closes in ten minutes and nothing much is going to be done by either of us until Monday. I'll be in touch.'

14

'I was followed from the bank.

'Not by the black-jacketed oaf I had spotted before but by an older man – fat, he looked like a minor clerk, a shop-walker in an unfashionable shop. His clothes were too small, did not button up properly. I imagined that he had been brought up by a hard-line Falangist and recruited or pushed into JONS in his adolescence. Probably, I thought, he spends his evenings and weekends harassing intellectuals and left-wingers at the behest of the Secret Police. Or fulfilling duties like the one he was presently engaged on. There is a vast pool of such people who can be relied on to turn out for anyone whose credentials declare them to be pillars of the regime.

'I wasn't that far off the truth. The only thing is, his duties go beyond mere harassment.

'All of which suddenly seemed fanciful as I watched him stumbling and gasping on to the platform at Alonso Martínez as the Línea Cinco train I had just managed to slip on to as the doors closed, pulled away from him.

'However, when I got back to Desengaño, it seemed likely my paranoia was justified.

'"Evita" was there.

'I don't think it's necessary for me to justify my friend's attachment to "Evita". He is handsome, dark, thin, fit, intelligent, capable of affection and passion. If he were a girl no one would think twice, except possibly her parents who would not want her chances on the marriage market spoiled by a liaison with an impoverished actor twice her age. That their relationship is ... was ... '

STOP.

'Can I go on?
'I have to.'

PLAY AND RECORD:

'That their relationship *was* often stormy, had as much misery in it as bliss, is neither here nor there. That sort of thing can happen, too, in heterosexual relationships. Indeed it can. Anyway, "Evita" was there.

'We call him "Evita" because he once ... achieved an amazing impersonation, and the nickname stuck. He claims to be a Montonero in exile. Perhaps he is. But it is a claim that gains him status in the *ambiente* in which he and Ramón move. *Moved.* And perhaps for that reason he keeps it up and it cannot easily be refuted. Certainly he comes from a well-to-do Buenos Aires family, and is doing research at the Madrid medical school. I need a drink.'

STOP.

Roberto moved like a zombie through the tiny, literally freezing flat. There was ice on the inside of the kitchen window. A nearby clock struck once, which was annoying. It struck once for half past twelve, for one o'clock, and for half past one. Without turning on the radio he had no idea which it was.

He suffered pains now in his lower abdomen – crab-like clutches at his gut, and his concentration was drifting more and more frequently.

Absurdly he thought: I will blindfold myself, go, as they say, to the bathroom, come out, take off the blindfold, then wrap myself in every blanket I can find and go to bed and sleep ...

But he heated water, slopped brandy into it and fought one foot in front of the other back through the hall where he noticed a line of dust and dead spiders marking the old position of the wardrobe he'd dragged in front of the outside door, and so back to his room and his tape-recorder.

PLAY AND RECORD:

'"Evita" was there. And Ramón of course...'

Ramón called from his room as he heard Roberto's key in the door. He was sitting at his actor's dressing-table slowly painting his face into a likeness of Richard Nixon whom he was to portray for the first time that night in a *café-teatro* off Barco. Juan 'Evita' Castillo was lying back on the narrow bed with his head propped high on the pillows. He was idly fingering a small silver pistol – snapping back the breech, clicking the trigger. The air was thick with cigarette smoke.

'Yes?'

'"Evita's" got news for you.'

'Evita' pointed the gun. Roberto flinched. Click.

'I wish you wouldn't do that.'

'Enrico Gunter.'

'Yes?' Roberto sat in the spare cane chair and it creaked. The room was so small and so cluttered his knees touched the bed. It stank too – of unwashed clothes and weeks of strong, cheap cigarettes. But at least it was warm – the round electric fire, set on its back under the dressing-table, saw to that.

'Enrico Gunter. Buenos Aires businessman. You could say cosmopolitan. He's been helping Astra to expand in South America. Has worked on links between Astra and Beretta. Has German friends, and relations, in Argentina.'

'An arms-dealer.'

'Not *dealing*. Manufacturing. But he's just a businessman. With a businessman's skills. He's a consultant. Advises firms who are thinking of working together but are suspicious of each other. Paves the way in little countries who want arms made on their own territory. Knows his way round the bureaucracies – who needs a kickback and how much. OK. It's arms he's into now, but it could be anything – agricultural machinery, he's set up a Mengele factory or two in his time, rainforest clearance, hydro-electrics. What comes out at the end is fees and commissions, the product is no concern of his.'

'How did you find out all this?'

'Evita' shrugged. 'It's still a small world – the South American bourgeoisie in Madrid. You know that. They like to gossip.'

He snapped the breech, pointed it again. Click.

'How long has he known ... ?'

'Señora Josefina González?' 'Evita's' tone was sarcastic. 'I really don't know. Hey. Ramón? How many rounds do you have for this toy?'

Richard Nixon swung round. The swooping nose, like a phallus with a grooved glans on the end, wobbled and fell off. Ramón said: 'Six. A magazine full.'

'This?'

'Yes.'

'Evita' slotted the tiny case up into the butt.

'It's not really enough you know. You should get some more. I mean it's only small calibre, utterly ineffective over ten metres – unless you get lucky and hit someone in the eye. To be sure of that you need to be able to spray the landscape.'

Ramón turned back to the mirror, manipulating the putty between his fingers. 'Difficult. It's old. German. Pin-fire two two. It's all rim-fire nowadays.'

'I'll get you some. Pepita. And Enrico. Difficult to say. He's been around in Madrid for more than a year. That circle being what it is he would have met her pretty soon. How long he's been fucking her is anybody's guess.'

He snapped the breech, pointed, and Roberto grabbed. The bang – short as a whiplash – was utterly shocking. They all looked at each other. Was any of them hurt? Apparently not. They began to giggle, then roar with laughter, and Ramón indicated the tiny hole in the ceiling. The smell of cordite spiced the other odours.

'I told you it was harmless,' heaved 'Evita', thrashing on the bed.

'And now there's only five,' shouted Ramón. 'There's something else,' he added.

'Evita' tried to wrestle for the gun but Roberto was firm, acting the role of the benign surrogate uncle.

'One lucky escape was enough. Something else?'

'Tell him, "Evita".'

'A top German Nazi, he's called Hans Adler, flew into Madrid three days ago. To honour the Caudillo and assist in the obsequies to come, he told the press. He's second generation, so can move about as he likes. But he called on an ex-*Azul* in the Security Police who told him where to find La Aguja.'

'The Needle?'

'The Needle.'

'Who is . . . ?'

'A hit man. A contract killer.'

Roberto felt cold in spite of the fug in the room. 'Fat? With glasses?'

'Yes. But he's over forty, a Cuban by birth. So, he has spectacles and he's fat. He is said to be SS trained.'

STOP.

A deep sigh.

PLAY AND RECORD:

'So I kept the pistol in my pocket. After that sort of news I would have been stupid not to. Later I hid it amongst my books.

'I asked: "Can you connect Gunter with these Nazis?"

'"Evita" replied: "Yes. Of course. I already have. He

has German connections, he's in business. Do I have to make any other connection?"

'"But nothing concrete. Nothing firm."

'"Evita"', not able to give a concrete answer, feigned boredom. He swivelled on to his hip and groped for another cheap black Canaries cigarette from the packet under the bed.

'"No."

'That was Saturday afternoon. Two days before the meeting at the Príncipe. No reason really not to continue with one's established routines. These, however, were interrupted. I was warned. Warned off. I should really have taken my cue. Of course I should. Ramón...'

15

Sunday morning. An elderly man struggled up out of the La Latina Metro, struggled because the crowd was quite dense although it was November, struggled because he was carrying two battered suitcases which had once had quality but which were far too heavy for him. A young boy, about twelve years old, his clothes patched and clearly handed down or bought on street kerbs, waited for him at the turnstiles.

Roberto straightened, gasped for air, rubbed the palms of his hands into the small of his back, then put his hand on the boy's shoulder. The boy put down the cases and waited.

'*Momento. Por favor.*' A little colour came back into his cheeks. He shook his head, wiped his hands then his face on a handkerchief. '*Buenos, Jaime, y gracias. Arriba. Vamos.*'

The boy hoisted the cases and followed Roberto up the last flight of stairs into the cold winter sunshine of the Plaza de Cascorro.

The Rastro, the flea market of Madrid, is for real. In summer the poverty is diluted by the tourists – Americans, Japanese, Arabs come in coaches, and the middle, even upper middle classes come down from Chamberí and Recoletos to pick up bargains: Castilian furniture made from hide studded on to black frames that weigh lighter than you expect when you pick them up, three-legged stools that weigh heavier; fans which claim to be hand-painted – and so they are, in sweat shop assembly line done by numbers, Talavera pottery, ditto; Toledo swords six inches or six feet long, all bearing the name of the sword of El Cid; antique pistols made the day before yesterday; all the paraphernalia of the Corrida from a full suit of lights to a paper-knife made like an *espada* and therefore impractical because of the bend at the tip; paintings of soulful virgins, and of soulful Virgins, of chubby Christs and of chubby little boys who wink over their shoulders while weeing in the gutter; paintings of Don Quixote and Sancho Panza done in the good old *costumbristic* style, ditto done spiky and modern with impasto inches deep; paintings there solely to advertise the ornate frames they are in. And, mostly at the top end of the area, not far from La Latina, books.

In summer the poverty is real, in winter it is obvious. A thin man sells an empty gas cylinder to buy food he will no longer be able to cook. An old man sells a chair because his room has no fireplace in which he might burn it. Old ladies in black with plastic bags in yellow and red carefully saved from trips to Simago bargain at the vegetable and fish stalls for produce gone limp and unwholesome since Friday morning when they first arrived in town.

And the books. Apart from a few second-hand bookshops in the narrow alleys off the Ribera de Curtidores these are mostly sold from trestled tables at the top end of the market: stacks of illustrated *folletines* and *novelas por entregas*, simplified translations of everything from *The Wandering Jew* to *War and Peace*, and none of them complete; similarly incomplete book-club sets of Pérez Galdós and Baroja; stacks of children's encyclopedias produced alphabetically as weekly magazines whose publishers went bust at *Manila-Mexico*.

Roberto took his usual pitch under a plane tree, little more than a sapling; Jaime took the *duro* he was paid for carrying the suitcases and promised to be back for another at two o'clock – assuming the elderly gentleman had not sold off his stock, ha, ha. Roberto unfastened the catches, undid the straps and spread his wares on the cobbles and the tiny scrap of earth under the tree. He sat on a tiny camping-stool. He was cold. He wore his black Homburg, his ancient Crombie, a grey muffler and woollen gloves cut down to make mittens, but still he was cold. There were very few buyers about and he wondered, as always, why he bothered. Out loud a Municipal Policeman wondered the same. Roberto shrugged, said nothing.

His life would have little purpose if he did not do it – that was why.

The policeman, a robust fat man, peered down at the books. He did not like what he saw. Most of them were paperbacks with rough edges where the pages had been cut. Some had fawn-coloured covers printed boldly with striking designs in black and faded red. Was that not a hammer and sickle? Was that not a clenched fist? And were not many of them printed in Barcelona and in a language that was not Castilian? A week ago Juan Carlos, as acting head of state, had signed an edict permitting Catalans to speak Catalan. But that surely did not mean that books in Catalan could be sold in the streets of Madrid. He wondered if he should use his lapel radio and consult his superiors, but he feared that he would be told off for being a fool. Anyway, the elderly gentleman looked very respectable with his close-clipped white moustache like the poor Caudillo's and his gold-framed spectacles.

Half an hour passed and the cold began to bite. Roberto stood and banged mittened hands together, then sat down again on his camping-stool. Two students, a girl and a boy, dressed in imitation of American students in donkey jackets, sweaters, jeans, and sneakers, but all, because they were Spanish, pressed and spotless, stooped and poked about in his pile and whispered with awe to each other at what they found. *The Civil War in France. The*

81

Origin of the Family. 'Jesus,' muttered the boy, 'it's dangerous to own even the *Origin of the Species*.' And they passed on.

Three more youths arrived, not too different from the students in appearance but with boots instead of sneakers and leather instead of duffel. They too poked about in Roberto's stock for a moment or two, peered into his face, checking they had the right man. Then they closed in and the one in the middle unzipped himself.

For a moment that seemed like a minute Roberto, on his stool with his head on a level with the uncircumcised, slightly tumescent prick, waited. Then the manipulated foreskin slid back and the stream, directed at his books, began. He snatched off his hat and swatted.

The other two lads moved in. They backhanded him across the face and his spectacles scuddered away across the cobbles. He groped after them. Then, not wanting to mark his face, they came in with their boots. They knew their trade. They aimed for the soft parts. There would be no broken bones, no blood. No external blood. When they had finished they lifted up the suitcases and tipped the books and pamphlets over him. The whole episode lasted two minutes at the most.

Roberto clutched at his heart. Or so it seemed. In fact he was protecting his spare, and now his only pair of spectacles, kept in an inside pocket, in an old-fashioned strengthened case.

Jaime, the street boy who earned ten pesetas every Sunday carrying Roberto's cases to and from La Latina had been told what was happening. Just as the other sellers and buyers were on the point of deciding that really it was no longer dangerous to see if the elderly gentleman needed help, he arrived. To everyone's relief the old man was persuaded to sit on his righted stool; he allowed Jaime to repack his suitcases; he allowed him to lead him back to the Metro.

82

16

The second warning came on Monday. Roberto, who had been beaten in the street twice before, recovered quite quickly. The actual injuries were painful enough certainly, but had left no internal lesions or haemorrhage. The worst thing about such events is the shock, the sense of outrage, the feeling of helplessness in the face of hostile forces one can do nothing about...

One reaction is an almost overpowering desire to stop in bed, to stay away from it all, keep out of sight. Roberto resisted this by giving himself a treat: breakfast in the Nebraska *cafetería* in Hortaleza, where he blew half the day's food and drink budget on chocolate and *churros*. After all, he was already two hundred dollars ahead of the game, and would presumably earn another hundred that evening. Three hundred dollars was a month's income.

So there he sat beneath warm spotlights, in a black leatherette chair watching with pleasure a pretty girl with a low-cut shirt which exposed deliciously the swelling creaminess of her breasts as she stooped to wipe the tables nearby. He listened with delight to an exchange between the older lady, fat and jewelled, who managed the Gaggia, and the tall, sallow barman. Prime Minister Carrero Blanco, blown up two years earlier while leaving a brothel now claimed his position in heaven would be senior to Franco's for he had left only a leg behind. While it seemed

Franco would be bringing only his head...

A young man, expensively dressed, immaculately groomed, came in, interrupted their snickers, asked a question, ordered a *café solo*, and, to Roberto's surprise since the *cafetería* was almost empty at this hour, came and joined him

'*Se puede?*'

Roberto signified assent. The young man placed his octagonal green cup on the table and distributed around himself a collapsible umbrella in a leather case, a pair of gloves, a scarf, and a soft leather purse with a wrist strap. Then, seated at last, he pushed long hairy fingers through wiry black hair (a gold ID bracelet glittered in the spotlight) and came finally to rest with his chin on his hands, and his elbows on either side of his coffee. He fixed Roberto with dark eyes, serious, concerned.

'Señor Fairrie?'

'*Sí.*'

'I am Private Secretary to the Marqués of Boltana, Don Antonio Pérez y Mendizábal. He is a director of the Bank of Corpus Cristi.'

'Really?'

'If it's no trouble for you, he would like to speak to you this morning on a matter of some importance.'

Roberto attempted to make a show of looking at his watch, a gold Rolex twenty years old, but he had sold it, and it was no longer there.

'Finish your breakfast, of course.'

'I intend to.' He dipped the penultimate *churro* in the thick, cinnamon-flavoured chocolate, sucked appreciatively at the grooved, drooping length of fast-fried doughnut paste, before relishing the crispness at the undipped end.

The Secretary sipped his coffee, grimaced. He had taken neither cream nor sugar, and clearly it was far too bitter.

'How did you know where to find me?'

'Your friend in your apartment said you might be here. The head office of the bank is in the Plaza de España, as I'm sure you know, opposite the Hotel El Príncipe. We can take a taxi.'

Roberto refused to be hurried. He slipped a couple of tissues from the dispenser on the table, wiped fingers and mouth with exaggerated care, took two more tissues and slipped them in his top pocket. Then he picked up the unused, still wrapped sugar lumps the Secretary had left. Remote cousins in England had done very well manufacturing little cubes of sugar. Through some commercial quirk these still carried his name on them.

The Marqués, seated at a desk that would not have disgraced an emperor, beneath windows which, had they been stained, would have graced a cathedral, welcomed, or at any rate acknowledged his presence, across half an acre of Aubusson. Roberto, bred into and by the upper bourgeoisie of Buenos Aires, was up to it. He stood in the doorway through which the Secretary had announced him, slowly took off his hat, gloves and muffler, and dropped them on a nearby chair, straightened one of the Nebraska's tissues in his breast pocket so just a dot of a white triangle appeared above the hem, and set off on the journey to the desk.

The Marqués leant back in his throne to watch his progress which was stiff, painful, and slow. Roberto did his utmost to disguise the pain, but it was not easy, and he felt he was not doing well.

Then he stopped. He couldn't help it. On the panelled wall, half-way down the room was a very large painting of an elegant eighteenth-century grandee dressed in scarlet and white with a blue and white sash. He was surrounded by *objets d'art* and in the foreground a smaller, darker figure held up a painting for the grandee to inspect. He, however, had eyes only for his portrait painter.

Roberto, arrested at first by sheer surprise, took the

opportunity to stay where he was and thus forced the Marqués to make the first move.

He cleared his throat. 'There is, as I am sure you know Señor Fairrie, a similar painting in the Urquijo Bank.'

'No better than this, Marqués,' said Roberto. 'And it was very rare indeed for Goya to do more than one version of a painting. Velázquez, on the other hand... '

'Well,' the Marqués was expansive, 'they both ran studios you know. Not quite factories perhaps, but they had assistants and so on. The Urquijo Bank's version is better known than ours, and they are much bothered by people asking to see it.'

The Marqués offered him a seat in front of the desk. There were three chairs set there round a low table. Roberto pointedly remained standing and eventually the Marqués came round the desk and took one of them. It was now possible for Roberto to see him properly. Until then his second pair of spectacles, not quite the same prescription as those smashed in the Rastro, together with the light flooding in behind the Marqués, had left his perception of the man vague.

What he now saw was not interesting. A well-set-up man, about his own age, with a figure once trim going to fat behind a perfectly cut silver-grey suit, a tanned face that shone, hair silver, wiry and brushed back, eyes and mouth mean, suspicious and bullying in repose, but capable of instant charm.

'It was good of you to come at such short notice. I will return the favour by coming straight to the point. You are an expert on the life of President Perón.'

'Yes.'

'Not well known as such. But still an expert.'

Roberto remained mute.

'And as we, I, understand it, you are at present employed by an American with Swiss nationality called Clemann to authenticate or otherwise a set of tapes that are on sale as the uncensored reminiscences of Perón.'

86

'Yes.'

'I take it that you know that a large set of tapes made by Perón here in Madrid were bought a year ago from Señora Nini Montiam, the actress, and will be published next year by Planeta? Possibly *ABC* may serialise some of the transcriptions.'

'Yes. I know that. That is public knowledge.'

The Marqués leant back, his eyes glittered narrowly over clasped fingers.

'Tell me, Señor Fairrie, you have heard some of this second set of tapes?'

'Two short extracts, yes.'

'And they are forgeries.'

This was said with finality. Roberto took his time.

'I have not yet made up my mind.'

'But I think you will say they are forgeries.'

'I doubt if I shall ever make a final assertion on the matter. Without scientific electronic voice analysis involving similar tape known not to be forged, no one is ever going to be able to say definitely, without a shadow of doubt one way or the other. What I have heard of the tapes so far is near enough like Perón's voice, near enough the sort of thing you might expect him to say, to make such analysis a necessity. Without it, one can only express opinion. Informed, expert opinion. But only opinion.'

'And your opinion?'

Roberto repeated: 'I have not yet made up my mind.'

The Marqués got up, moved behind his chair to the side of his desk and so to the tall window furthest from Roberto. His head sank a little between his shoulders, his podgy fingers were clasped behind his back where they fidgeted and flexed.

'I gather you had an unfortunate experience in the Rastro yesterday morning.'

The Marqués's eyes remained fixed on the Cervantes monument below.

Roberto's gut shrivelled with fury and fear.

'And I suppose your permit of residence must run out some time in the next few months. I imagine you will not find the regime in your own country very congenial. And when it falls, the sort that will take over will be not so much uncongenial to you as positively dangerous. Really, Señor Fairrie, it does seem to me, on the face of it virtually certain, even without scientific analysis, that these new tapes are forgeries, and your duty is to expose them as such. Well. I mustn't keep you. You are, I am sure, a busy man.'

This was a sneer. The podgy Marqués, framed in the window, drew out a long thin cigar, and snapped a flame at it. Sweating with rage, chagrin, and terror, Roberto stumbled and limped back to the big door, collected his outdoor garments and went.

The Marqués did not move, did not acknowledge his departure.

17

Again Roberto stopped the tape. This time what was happening in his lower gut would not be denied. The only bucket in the attic flat was overflowing with garbage. Later he realised he could have tipped this into plastic bags but with his head swimming with brandy and sleeplessness, his limbs almost paralysed with cold, it did not occur to him. And so he blundered at last, eyes averted, into the bathroom but was forced to turn round to sit on the bowl. He evacuated evil-smelling diarrhoea and waited to enjoy the release from pain. Inevitably he looked at the obscenely masked cadaver of his friend. He had never seen the body naked before – he regretted this deeply, to the point of renewed weeping, that the wholesomeness of familiarity with the living flesh of a man he had loved had been denied to him by the absurd restrictions of a 'civilisation' he had devoted most of his life to trying to undermine, subvert. He should have known better. That was the trouble. No matter how hard he had tried to reject all that he hated, it was congenital, introjected, inescapable. Marcuse and Lukács, and many others, in very different ways, had written about this. It was something he had not given enough thought to.

Then something horrible happened. His friend was gone, but movement, even life went on, though no longer the life of his friend. Hair and nails grow after death. Less pleasant things happen too.

The cadaver farted. The bubbles burst in discoloured water above its crotch.

Roberto vomited again – everything, it seemed, that he had eaten and drunk since he came in. Then he managed to get to the kitchen where he boiled a saucepan of water. This he emptied into a jug, and from the jug he poured the hot water into a litre-sized Casera lemonade bottle with a porcelain and wire top. He closed the top. Then he collected every blanket he could find, using Ramón's as well as his own, and, stripped to his long underwear, with his improvised hot-water bottle, rolled himself up on his own bed. The clock struck twice just as he was sinking into a short but very deep sleep.

Later he woke and half dreamed, half dozed, half consciously recollected a variety of things. Buenos Aires – wide streets and high buildings, acacias and plane trees, drums remorselessly beating in tango rhythm to punctuate the flow of speeches mouthed from a balcony, hideously amplified by loudspeakers. Evita – pale hair, skin glowing unnaturally, driven through the streets at Perón's second inauguration, with, they said, a steel ramrod up her back to keep her upright.

He dreamt too of, or remembered, a wife. A lovely woman. She had come to his arms with glee and together they made a child as beautiful as she. But she had not liked his bookshop, his friends, above all she had not liked the raids the police occasionally made on them. They separated. And confused with her he dwelt on the sudden totally unexpected bliss of bed with Becky Herzer – and here something niggled, worried, nagged. Why had she done it? Why? Though not a vain man, Roberto had his share of masculine vanity, and only now did it occur to him to ask: why?

He twisted and turned, forced himself a little more awake, and acknowledged as the memory of it all became sharper, that of course he knew why. It had been quite

90

clear. And in gratitude he had made her a promise, a promise he would no longer have to keep. Nevertheless something nagged again. If Cockburn had not asked Herzer to come back to Madrid, had not told her about the new tapes, then who had?

He dozed on, woke in a dim light filtered between the slats of the built-in roller blind that covered his window. Not bright enough to wake him, so what had? The guns and the bell. The monotonous thud of the field guns in the Parque del Oeste took up again their dreary salute to the dead dictator, and the nearer, muffled clang of the church of San Martín a couple of hundred metres down the road.

The security, almost a numb sense of contentment, that had built up with his body warmth evaporated as quickly as the warmth itself. Anxiety, as sharp as fear bit into him, and for a moment or two he sucked and chewed on his thumb and whimpered.

But he got up, attempting briskness though his bruised organs would not allow it, put on trousers, a cardigan, a long flannel dressing-gown, his muffler and mittens. Then he made himself coffee again, and finished the stale bread. Back in his room he sat himself in front of the tape-recorder, pressed the play and record buttons, then stopped them again.

He reached for the radio and caught the end of an announcement. Don Juan Carlos de Borbón will be sworn in as King and Head of State in front of the Cortes at noon. He will then address the Cortes and the nation. Roberto thought – well, if nothing has happened here by then, I'll listen to that. Meanwhile news bulletins will follow every hour on the hour, and in between solemn music...

The Eroica! The Eroica symphony for that cadaver in the *Palacio Real*, and all the man had been and done! Napoleon even was a more suitable dedicatee! Still, not too often did one hear Beethoven on Spanish radio, it was an added bonus when evil men were allowed at last to die.

Could he continue to tape his version of the events that

had led to two murders with the music on too? Well, he had a small set of headphones, and he could try, with the volume turned low.

PLAY AND RECORD:

'I arrived at the Príncipe at eight o'clock on Monday evening, sparing a curse for the Banco de Corpus Cristi on the other side of the Cervantes monument.

'Professor McCabe was sitting in an armchair in the foyer and he rose to greet me.

'"I thought I'd wait for you. We can go up together."

'In the lift he asked me what I thought about the whole business. I was non-committal. He said he was inclined to think the tapes were forgeries and that the swindle had been set up by Señora González and Cockburn. Nevertheless they were good forgeries, other people must have been involved as well. He added that he was talking about no more than inclination, instinct. He'd have to hear a lot more tape.

'I agreed: that from my point of view that was a necessity too – without electronic analysis, which I still hoped would be forthcoming, I should want to hear a lot more tape before offering a firm opinion.

'We knocked on the door of Steve Cockburn's room, and he let us in.

'The room was of course relatively small, and, to my dismay, thick with smoke. The two twin beds had been pushed together against the wall. On them sat Swivel, an American-trained Swiss lawyer, and Becky Herzer.

'Swivel is podgy, indeed fat. He was in his waistcoat with shirt collar unbuttoned above a loosened tie, one of those striped ones the English wear to show they belong to something. He has thick, moist lips, sharp eyes, and is no more than thirty years old. In answer to a nod from Clemann he went out into the corridor and came back with two upright chairs.

'Herzer, Becky, on this occasion wore a white blouse

with expensive lace beneath a black velvet pinafore, black court shoes, jet necklace, and carried her glasses suspended from a silk noose.

'There was a bucket of nearly melted ice and a litre bottle of duty-free Glenlivet three-quarters gone. McCabe and I were offered a meagre finger each in hotel toothmugs.

'During the discussion that followed Swivel took notes, in a small hard-backed notebook. He did not use shorthand. Lawyers learn to take very complete notes in longhand. I felt I should be careful, anything I said was being taken down, and ... '

'I think I should fill you in on what has happened since we last met,' said Clemann – leaning forward over his knees, so his face with his large glasses framed in black, rocked between McCabe's and Roberto's in a way that Roberto found too close for comfort. 'Briefly, aware as I am that Señora González would like us to think that she has put us in a privileged position because of her relationship with Steve, and her knowledge through the last set of negotiations with Señora Montiam of his connection and friendship with me, and that this privilege has a limited date set to it, I used my influence with, and knowledge of, Spanish finance to make contact with the owners of the *ABC* tapes during the afternoon and evening of Saturday, although of course business houses were officially closed.'

The brisk but complex way this was put indicated to Roberto a little more what sort of man Clemann was. Not a fool, except in so far as he believed that those he paid would respond with the sort of intelligence he had to whatever he said.

'I asked them to release ten minutes of their tape so we could use it as a sample in an electronic voice test. Late on Saturday evening I received a very firm refusal. Henry was about to give his assessment of this when you arrived.' He swung his head towards the fat lawyer. 'Perhaps you'd like to take it on from there.'

'Sure.' Swivel was smoking a small cheroot and he now ground the end in the glazed pottery ashtray that bore the arms of the nineteenth-century Borbon prince whose palace the hotel had once been. He spoke with an accent that very nicely blended Swiss-German with American law school. 'There was no way the owners of the *ABC* tapes would let you use a sample in that way...'

Clemann: 'I did not mean them to know how it would be used. I just offered a large sum for a small sample.'

Cockburn: 'That's not exactly how it was. I was the one on the blower. First they refused outright. Then I offered the top fee you would be prepared to pay. They came back three hours later and suggested that we wanted the tape so we could compare it with other tape. I have to say, I believe they had somehow found out why you, we, wanted that sample. I suspect that my denial was half-hearted.'

Roberto thought: So the street beating and the Marqués of Boltana happened because of Cockburn's clumsiness.

Swivel, meanwhile: 'So. As I said. No way would they give you a sample. Consider. If the voice test proved your tapes the same as theirs, they are blown. Yours are far more sensational, you'd take the market, no one would buy the *ABC* tapes once yours were out.'

Clemann: 'They don't know ours are more sensational.'

Cockburn: 'Not ours yet.'

'Anyway,' said Swivel, 'they'd sense competition they had no reason to welcome. On the other hand, if the analysis showed a mismatch the way would be open for you to say yours were the right ones and theirs the forgery. All of you heard some of the tape *ABC* now has. Or the people *ABC* are fronting for. You say the quality of recording was awful. On grounds of voice alone there was no way of asserting they were authentic. There was background noise, hiss, distortion. It could have been Charlie Chaplin doing the Great Dictator.' He lit another cheroot taken from a tin with a picture of Tom Thumb on it and blew a cloud of new smoke through the layers about his head. 'OK. You accepted their authenticity, and so did the *ABC* buyers. For why? Because Nini Montiam's credentials were impeccable, and because the content fitted. McCabe here was sent transcriptions and he agreed the content...'

McCabe nodded slow agreement.

'Now, however, you have a set of tapes, one of which at any rate dates from the same period as the first ones, but a very good quality recording, the voice apparently accurate, and the content though sensational, apparently credible. At least not to be thrown out of court. If, as I say, there was a mismatch, and no foolproof scientific evidence available, and if it came to a legal dispute, the owners of the *ABC* tapes might well lose. And for sure they'd have to spend a lot of money. And, too, they know that for as long as Clemann is buying the second tapes, there is an awful lot of money if he chooses to use it to go on fighting court-cases for ever. No. No way are *ABC* going to lend you sample tape for comparative analysis. No way.'

Clemann turned to Herzer.

'Is there anyone else we can get an authentic sample from?'

Herzer leaned forward and her glasses swung beneath her chest. She clasped her fingers in front of them and made brisk double-fisted gestures. To Roberto it seemed as if she had managed somehow to unsex herself.

'Not easy,' she said. 'The regime that ousted Perón in '55 tried to destroy the Perón myth. All recordings of his speeches, together with a mass of other material, was destroyed or hidden. The recent stuff is controlled by Isabelita. She is not going to release anything without very firm assurances that it can't be used in any way to damage Peronismo or her.' She recrossed her ankles. 'But there are agencies and privately run archives – firms that keep sound, video and filmstock to hire out. I know of a couple that might have some Perón and one is in Barcelona. They know me. I'll be in touch with them first thing in the morning.'

'That sounds hopeful,' said Clemann.

Swivel shook his big head morosely.

'I don't see it,' he said. '*ABC* or whoever is behind them are on to you now. They'll have leverage in Barcelona. Any firm, any private firm that has Perón tapes will be strongly pressured to deny it for the next few weeks – you'll see. You should have gone to the libraries first, not alerted *ABC*.'

Cockburn, his arm up on the high-backed chair, said: 'So. We're back with our experts. At least that's what it looks like. And if we don't buy by the end of the week González will go elsewhere, and I don't see us getting a voice test off the ground by then.'

They all looked at Roberto and McCabe, neither of whom seemed ready to say anything. Then McCabe cleared his throat: 'If you mean you want us to give a guaranteed certificate of authenticity or an equally firm thumbs down, then I for one, and I think Señor Fairrie agrees with me, I am just not going to be able to do that.'

Cockburn was insistent – face serious, dark eyes intent: 'But surely the more you hear, the more certain either way you can become.'

'Oh sure. Give us a matter of some hours, preferably listening to the lot, and I reckon I could then give a pretty definite assurance one way or the other. Pretty definite, and subject only to being proved wrong by an objective scientific test. You see, when the chips are down, it's content that counts. Could a forger go on for some hours without dropping into some crass and entirely provable error? I doubt it.'

'Señor Fairrie?'

'Up to a point, Mr Cockburn, Steve, I agree with Professor McCabe. I'm not too sure though about his emphasis on fact. Apart from anything else Perón was an inveterate liar. If there were no lies at all in the tapes, then I might doubt them quite seriously.'

McCabe was edgy: 'There's fact and fact, content and content. I accept what you say about Perón's veracity. What I shall be looking out for rather more carefully is little errors about *him*. For instance in that last extract we heard him apparently light a cigarette. But was he a smoker . . . ?'

While Roberto was still reacting, McCabe cut him off and went on: 'Yes, he was. Fine. But if he had not been a smoker, then there. Those tapes were blown. That's really the sort of content I'm looking for all the time. And that's why I want to hear a heck of a lot more tape.'

Clemann: 'Steve. Do you think González will go along with that – give McCabe and Fairrie a chance to hear the lot? Eight cassettes, supposing them to be fully used C90s is twelve hours plus, leave alone the spool-to-spool stuff, which could be recorded double for all we know.'

Cockburn shrugged. 'We can but try. But there will be problems with the bank. I suspect they might not like us taking out squatters' rights on their vault.'

'She could try asking them to let her use it after hours. Or she could take the goddamn things out and play them here or at her flat. I would pay for some goons to guard them.' Clemann suddenly stretched his arms above his head, then stood up. Coming from a low chair in a small room, Roberto thought the process would go on for ever. The tall American exile moved through the chairs to a marble mantelpiece above what was now a filled-in fireplace with an electric fire. He turned, rested his elbows on the high shelf, and looked down at them all. 'I think that's as far as we can go tonight. Becky. Tomorrow morning you use the phone here on my account to get round any of those agencies or archives you think might have tape. Steve, you get González to give us a proper audition of a substantial section of tape. Professor, Señor Fairrie, Cockburn will be in touch with you as soon as he's fixed that up. Your fees are a hundred dollars for the first hour and a further hundred for every part of an hour thereafter. Henry will pay you cash at the end of every session. At the end of the whole business, whatever the outcome, you give him a digest of your expenses with receipts for bills above twenty dollars.

'Now. I want you all to understand that my initial reaction to these tapes remains the same. The set-up stinks. On the question of their authenticity I fear both our experts have got it a bit wrong, and Henry has got it right... '

Swivel smirked.

'... If I buy a Monet, I don't go to Clark or whoever, I check out the provenance, a family tree of who owned the picture right back to Claude's studio. So. Steve, you have to go back to González on this question too, with Henry, and tell her she comes clean about provenance, and title, before we move a step further. As Henry says, the provenance of the *ABC* tapes is impeccable. That for these has to be at least as good. She's said she wants money before she reveals provenance. OK. The first thing that happens is this. She explains the provenance to us, to all of us. If our experts agree it looks good, then, there and then Henry gives her $2,000 and we go ahead and hear more tape. If our experts don't like her story, then we give her $1,000 for the trouble we've caused her and we all go home. Henry, I leave it to you to set this up, with Steve liaising between you and González, or whatever representative she chooses to appoint. I imagine we might meet again at this stage the Gunter character you told me about.

'But even if provenance looks good, I'm still not at all sure we shall be able to publish. Clearly a lot of people are going to go to considerable lengths to stop publication. And I am absolutely not interested in the tapes for any other reason than to publish.

'Worst of all, it all feels to me that Señora González is using us precisely in the same way as we were used before –

using our interest and the clout of my money to jack up the price to buyers already in the market.

'So. Unless our experts agree on the authenticity of these tapes, and unless we are satisfied as to their provenance and González's title to them, by two o'clock Wednesday when the banks close, I'll be on the evening plane back to Geneva. Right. Any brief comment or questions?'

McCabe cleared his throat. 'I find your consultancy fee fine in itself. But I do not take it that you expect for that for me to be on call in Madrid until this affair is settled.'

'I do. You want a retainer fee? Five hundred dollars a week.'

'For the first week. After that...'

'Professor, I pay people to bargain for me. See Henry about it. But I would suggest you recall that I do not intend to be in Madrid beyond Friday. Señor Fairrie. Do you want a retainer?'

Roberto thought, then said: 'No. But I should like you to understand that I entirely accept the importance of provenance; if Señora González can convince me in that respect, I shall feel far readier to endorse the tapes.'

Becky Herzer, unharnessed her spectacles and folded them away into a soft leather purse: 'Of course. Señor Fairrie is right. It is the question I asked at the first meeting at the bank. Where did these tapes come from?'

Swivel closed his notebook, snapped an elastic band over it. All stood up, stretched, brushed off tobacco ash, bumped into each other. Cockburn held the door open for McCabe and Roberto. 'I'll see you to the door. Organise a taxi.'

In the lift he went on: 'I don't think you should take too seriously Peter's threats about pushing off on Wednesday. Pepita is pressing him. So he's pressing back. Standard business practice.' He asked where they could be found the next morning. McCabe would stay indoors at his hotel, the Wellington. What else was a retainer for? Roberto was going to the National Library in the morning. But first he would phone in between ten and eleven to see what was happening.

18

Roberto had a large Mahou beer and a toasted ham and cheese sandwich at the Nebraska in Hortaleza to celebrate the increase to his exchequer. As he came out into the cold, frosty, starry night he could see beneath the street lights Richard Nixon and his wife coming down the pavement towards him.

Tricky Dicky was in front, walking briskly, head down, with thinning sleeked black hair, the nose swinging like an ant-eater's, almost, it seemed, sensing the scraps in the gutter. His wife, on high heels, clacked behind and was screaming at him in furious Spanish...

'It's always the same. You take on too much. You're a fucking Utopian. A Quixote. When you run out of giants, you look for Turks. It was crazy to do this at this time. I'm through. If you think I'm staying...'

Nixon stopped in front of Roberto.

'Roberto? You shouldn't be on the streets at this time of night. They're not safe.'

Ramón pulled the nose off, rolled it into a ball, took his friend's elbow. Nixon's face, with Ramón's nose.

Mrs Nixon came up on Roberto's other side, pulled off the ash-blond wig, revealed Juan 'Evita's' sleek, short, black hair.

'What happened?' Roberto asked. 'I did not expect you home so soon.'

'Fucking police raided us,' cried Juan 'Evita'. 'Just before the end of the first performance. Paulino bundled us out through the window of the ladies' toilet, as the pigs came in the front.' He stopped, twisted, lifted his skirt. '*And* one of my stockings has run. Ramón, you'll pay for this. You really are a silly, silly cunt.'

'You didn't have to...'

'Didn't have to? No. I said I wouldn't. But that wasn't enough. You pleaded. You wept. And silly cow that I am, I gave in. But that's it. I'm through now.'

They swung into Desengaño and Juan 'Evita's' foot twisted on the kerb.

'Shit and fucking hell!' He hobbled, stooped, plucked off his shoes and trotted after them, skirts swinging, beads clacking, catching them as they turned into the *pensión* entrance.

'You know, Ramón, I could brain you with these shoes. I could have your balls off...'

Ramón turned on the stairs.

'Jesus, "Evita". Shut up. Go home. Piss off. I've heard enough.'

'Go home? In these rags? Just let me remind you there's a law against female impersonation in this arsehole of a city. I've got clothes up there and I'm going to change into them, and then take everything else you've got of mine, what you haven't sold in the Rastro...'

Smack.

Ramón hit him. Not very hard, but very definitely a very significant gesture. For a moment their eyes blazed at each other, seething with energy and emotion, then they went on up the stairs with Roberto panting behind.

'I went to my room, Ramón stood in the kitchen doorway, Juan "Evita" stormed about in Ramón's room banging drawers and then the wardrobe in the hall. The one I've pulled in front of the outside door...'

'Don't expect me back. I've left the dress and wigs and all that crap. But I've taken everything that's really mine.' He hesitated for a moment, perhaps waiting for Ramón to climb down, apologise for the slap, take responsibility for the whole scene. But Ramón, still for the most part Richard Nixon, glowered above the cigarette he'd lit. Juan 'Evita' turned on his heeled boot and the flares of his low-slung trousers swung like a flamenco dancer's. He went.

Ramón stubbed his cigarette on a dirty plate and went to his room. Roberto waited a moment and then followed him in. Ramón was sitting at his mirrored table cleaning Nixon off his face. Already the toupee had gone revealing his *en brosse* grey hair with the hair line shaved back to match that of the ex-President. His eyes watered – with sadness, not the peeling away of gum arabic.

'He's right, Roberto. Not only female impersonation, but also impersonation of the head of a friendly state even when he is a crook, a war criminal, and no longer head of state. And this is not the time to be in a Spanish jail on charges that smack of deviance and dissidence. I should never have done this act. And I certainly should not have dragged him into it.'

'I think you worry too much about "Evita".'

'Not so. I still have a Spanish passport. But he, like you, can be deported. And in Argentina he may be wanted as a Montonero. And that means death. The Pinochets are taking over. Have you heard of General Videla?'

'Of course.'

'When Isabelita goes, he'll be in. And it will be worse than Chile. Anyway. How did it go with you?'

'All right. There's a problem or two, but nothing we can't deal with.' Roberto's voice was a touch plaintive. 'We thought this might happen, you remember?'

Cotton wool tossed into the tin waste-paper basket. 'I need a wash.'

Ramón got up, went to the bathroom, peeled off his shirt, dipped his head above the running taps. Roberto stood behind him. Ramón scrubbed at his face and swilled. The gas-heater banged and flared, and the fumes swung round them. Then he grabbed a threadbare towel, dried face, neck, hairy forearms.

'And I need a rest. I'm upset, you know?'

'Of course.'

'Tomorrow, eh? After all it seems I'm out of work again. In the morning, if you like.'

'In the morning. Later if you like. I'll leave you a draft, we can work on it in the evening. There's time.'

Ramón turned, patted Roberto on the shoulder, went through to his own room. Then called: 'Oh yes. Before "Evita" and I started shouting at each other he told me something you ought to know. You won't like it though.'

Roberto came to his door. Ramón was already on his bed looking up through the smoke of the cigarette he'd lit.

'La Aguja. Francisco Xavier Betelmann. And Don Martín. You know, so far eight people have died trying to prove Don Martín is alive and well and living in Argentina. Or Paraguay. Or Chile. Or wherever. And three of those times La Aguja, the Needle, was there or thereabouts. That's the gossip anyway. The sort of gossip "Evita" hears.' He stubbed out the cigarette, turned on the tiny unmade bed so the springs rang, pulled up the covers, and reached for the light-switch.

Roberto went to his own room, but heard Ramón call: 'And he's fat, middle-aged, and wears spectacles.' Nevertheless he pulled paper towards him and began to write, quickly, with confidence, only occasionally pausing to check with a reference book. Like many Spanish and Hispanic brain-workers he did his best work between midnight and two in the morning, and, provided he did not have to get up too early, felt none the worse for it.

19

'The next morning at about half past ten I phoned the Príncipe and was told by Cockburn that hitches had occurred. Herzer was trying to find sample tape, had had no luck with the Barcelona firm, and, more important, González had said there was no question of playing the tapes that day. She was booked, he said, to give another prospective buyer a hearing. Clemann, far from pleased, had agreed to attend, with his experts, on the morrow at noon, on condition that she revealed the provenance of her tapes and established title under terms agreed between them.

'I confess this was a relief in a way. After so much excitement I was ready to spend a relaxing day at the Biblioteca with Marañon's biography of Antonio Pérez. But of course that sort of plan or expectation never falls out. First, when I got off the Metro at Colón, I suffered a disagreeable experience.

'The Colón station is a terrible mess at the moment, because of the massive alterations going on both above and below ground. To get from the platforms to the surface one has to brave long, narrow tunnels with board walls, the infernal racket of construction machinery, and the rudeness of harassed officials and overstretched workmen.

'The boarded walls are an irresistible temptation to the agitprop activists of both left and right, and on one corner I found myself jammed in a small knot of people watching a young girl and boy, students perhaps, aerosoling out a message from the *Partido Español Nacional-Socialistica* much decorated with swastikas which they cleverly and neatly converted into the Anarchist 'A' in a circle. But then there was a clattering of boots down the long passage and four or five hooligans burst through us – I received a savage blow in my still bruised and painful chest. They were ruthless and the scene was ugly. I hurried as well as I could up the slopes and steps to the chill daylight but the screams of the girl, amplified by the passages, almost drowned out the machine-gun-fire of masonry drills, rang in my ears for most of the rest of the morning.

'I was ashamed too. Twenty, thirty years ago when that sort of incident occurred, I was not afraid to join in, and was sometimes beaten for my pains. This time I lacked even the courage to report the incident to a pair of Policia Armada who stood at the exit to the Metro. Not that that would have done much good. Probably they would have added arrest and another beating to what those brave children had already suffered.

'The library was warm and a temporary comfort. After negotiating the tedious checks and double checks I at last reached the reading-room – a pleasant hall, well but not garishly lit, decorated in cream marble and with bronze embellishments on the cases and reading lights, and they kept me waiting for less than twenty minutes before the book was brought to me.

'The tale, however, now lacked charm. Antonio Pérez had fallen from favour through his connection with the disastrous Princess of Eboli, was a wanderer now through Henry IV's Béarn, Elizabeth's England, and Paris – an ageing man without glamour or influence, constantly afraid of assassination from his old master Philip II. Philip

III turned out to be no better. Not long before he died he refused to see a fashionable rope-dancer, saying: "I have danced on the rope myself, and I have seen dancers fall to the ground with their limbs broken. I broke my back at it, there is too much danger and I am afraid." It all reminded me too vividly of my own situation, and at a little after midday I decided after all to go for a walk. Since the Bank of the Victory of the Angels is scarcely six blocks from the library it is not surprising that I found myself in its vicinity . . . '

Anyone observing Roberto's progress from the library to the bank, and there were in fact two men following him, would have detected nothing casual in his movements. He walked directly and briskly and only when he came in sight of the bank did uncertainty creep into his manner. For a time he hovered between two small plane trees, hung about the newspaper kiosk but did not buy anything, and finally walked fifty metres or so to a bus-stop where he waited, though he did not board the buses when they came. He remained there for over twenty minutes until at about ten to one a small party appeared on the steps of the bank. They included Señora González, Enrico Gunter, two middle-aged men in dark overcoats, and Becky Herzer. González and Gunter turned up the street, away from Roberto, towards González's apartment. Herzer and the two men in overcoats came towards Roberto but stopped fifteen metres before the bus-stop in front of a Mercedes and a Renault 12 with French number plates parked in echelon. The men shook hands briefly with Herzer and let themselves into the Mercedes. Herzer stooped, with her key feeling for the door of the Renault, straightened, face pale and blank, then suddenly smiling.

'Señor Fairrie?' She came towards him. 'What brings you here?'

He explained: he had been to the library, felt he had needed a change and had gone out for a walk, found the air more chill than he had expected, and was now waiting for a bus to take him back to the city centre where he had some shopping to do.

'A coincidence, merely?'

'Hardly. The library is very close.'

She laughed. 'Come. I was curious too, so why not admit it yourself? When Steve told me Señora González was entertaining further prospective buyers this morning, I discovered an urgent need to change some traveller's cheques.'

Her candour was disarming, the openness of her smile, creasing the soft brown skin round her eyes and wide mouth, enchanting. She had dropped the severe, executive appearance of the previous evening, was dressed in a long brown soft leather coat, with fur-topped boots that reached almost to its hem. Her near-white short hair was fluffed up beneath a Balmain scarf, and her cheeks glowed – with the cold after the warmth of the bank, perhaps.

'Don't you want to hear what I discovered? Of course you do. Well. The answer is... not much.' She laughed again. 'Of course it was embarrassing. They came up from the vault just as the cashier was giving me my pesetas. Nothing for it but to face it out. Introductions. Not all necessary, for I already know one of the men. I can give you a lift to Sol if you like.'

She unlocked the Renault, leant across to release the catch on the passenger's door. Inside Roberto was immediately conscious of the sharp and faintly feline pungency of her perfume. As she reversed the car into the carriageway she twisted to look over her shoulder and her face came very close to Roberto's. The sudden intimacy quite shook him. No doubt at all, she was a very attractive woman, and her age was an irrelevance.

'Well. Surely you wish me to tell you who he was?'

He agreed awkwardly that yes, though it really was no concern of his, it would be interesting to know.

'His name is Franz Rudel – I believe a connection of the *Luftwaffe* ace – and he is a banker in a house that has a lot of South American business. Clearly he knows Gunter well.'

'And the other?'

'Him I did not know previously. Herr Adler.'

She coped with the Madrid lunch-time rush hour traffic competently, even competitively.

'If I have this Adler placed properly in my mind he has a Bolivian passport.'

Roberto surreptitiously felt for the tissues still stuck in his top pocket and wiped perspiration from his palms. 'How do you know all this. All this about people like that?'

She shrugged without taking her eyes off the road. 'I am what Steve calls an international media person, you know? At bottom I am a journalist. I have been around a long time and it is the sort of area I specialise in. I think we should talk a little longer if you are not in a hurry. The shops will be open for a little longer yet.'

'All right.'

She turned down the Paseo del Prado, took a left turn, and parked near the Naval Museum. As always her movements were brisk, decisive, efficient. He was disappointed though when she shook out a cigarette and lit it with her tortoiseshell lighter.

'I cannot understand' – smoke streamed from her nostrils – 'why such people should be interested in the Perón tapes.'

'I suppose because of the bit about Bormann coming to visit him after his return to power.'

'Perhaps. But the rest... poof! Oh, it's all very interesting, perhaps will sell, make us all, as Steve would say, a bob or two. But I cannot see why people like Rudel and Adler should be here. Unless of course it is not the Perón tapes they are interested in. There are five cassettes that have nothing to do with Perón, according to Señora González. What is on those tapes, Señor Fairrie? I am sure you know.'

'No, indeed I do not.'

'You surprise me. For I think you know more about these tapes than you are prepared to say. Is that not the case?'

'No, really Madame Herzer. You do me an injustice. I am simply, fortuitously, an acquaintance of Cockburn's, and I happen to be the expert on Perón he needed in Madrid.'

'So he says. So you say. But, forgive ... you are hardly known widely as such. You are though known amongst the older generation of South American exiles as a staunch, indeed devout socialist, anti-fascist, and life-long opponent of the Peróns.'

This was all said lightly, even teasingly. Roberto was able to shrug off any implication that he had been less than frank.

'That is entirely true,' he said, 'and I have made it my business, the business of a lifetime, to understand what I so strongly oppose. I really doubt if anyone knows as much about the Peróns as I do. Not even the egregious Professor McCabe.'

She laughed. 'All right, Señor Fairrie, I must believe you. Now. Shall I take you to Puerta del Sol?'

'Please.'

Once there he groped for the catch on the door, could not find it, and she reached across him, her shoulder brushing his chest, her hair his cheek, and he felt again the sharp urgency of desire.

As she straightened she said: 'And you really do know nothing of these five extra cassettes?'

'Nothing. I assure you.'

This was said with entire frankness ...

'Rudel and Adler. Adler – what did "Evita" call him? A top Nazi. It was the third warning. Dear Lord, I should have re-

110

alised then, my very hormones, glands, whatever, if not my addled reason, were telling me. I was frightened when I got out of Becky's car. Very frightened. And with good cause, dear Lord, with good cause . . . '

20

At twelve o'clock the following day, Wednesday, they were all again in the vault of the Banco de la Victoria de los Angeles. All – Señora González had Enrico Gunter with her; Clemann had Cockburn, Herzer and Swivel in tow; and the experts – McCabe and Roberto. It made the room very crowded, extra chairs had been brought in. The cadaverous manager was clearly edgy about it. The most he would allow them was the hour and a half to closing time, and if any other customer wanted to use the vault during that time then they would have to clear out and move back later.

González, not in black this time, but in dark green wild silk with black star sapphires at her neck and in her ears, looked round them all slowly, fixing her gaze on Clemann with eyes that picked up the colour of her dress.

'First,' she said, 'you want provenance. I have agreed terms with Mr Swivel. Four thousand dollars now, in cash, if our experts are happy with what I say, and nothing at all if they are not. You have the money here?'

'Er, yes.' Swivel shifted uneasily, tapped a black document case that stood on the floor at his side.

'Señor Fairrie. As one of the two entirely independent people here, will you check the case for me?'

Roberto, surprised, but pleased to be singled out, stood up. The operation was not easy. Swivel had fastened the case to himself with a thin but clearly serviceable tungsten chain, and the keys to the case and chain were in the trouser pocket on the same side. Embarrassed, as embarrassed as Swivel himself, Roberto retrieved them. The case was opened.

'Señora, the money is here. I am not of course qualified to assess...'

Clemann was angry. 'Come *on*. This will not do. I am not the sort of person to give short change or pass forged bills.'

'Of course not.' González was soothing. 'Well then.' She paused while Swivel and Roberto returned to base. 'Well then. Provenance. You have already heard in this room the name López Rega mentioned. Someone described him as a member of the Perón entourage. He was a lot more than that. Perhaps Professor McCabe would like to tell us just who José López Rega was.'

'Me? Sure. Yes. Why not?' McCabe snapped shut his notebook, passed a mottled hand across his thinning hair, recrossed his legs. 'Yes indeed. He was far more than that. Really I don't know where to begin.'

Clemann: 'Keep it short. Just what is relevant.'

'Right.' McCabe made a church of his finger tips, thought for a moment, then: 'José López Rega was a police corporal, and for a time one of Perón's bodyguards during the second presidency. After the ouster of '55 he disappeared from the scene. Apparently he resigned the police force, and attempted to make a living as a spiritualist, a medium, that sort of thing. Then in 1966 Isabelita, Perón's third wife, now the President, went to Argentina...'

'Sixty-five.'

'Yes?'

Roberto insisted: 'She left here in '65, came back in '66.'

'Yes, yes. You're right. Anyway. While she was in Buenos Aires this López Rega got on to her staff as a baggage-handler, bodyguard, that sort of thing, and she brought him back here. Somehow or other, some would say by occult means, he gained a very complete ascendancy over her, and, either on his own account or through her, over Perón as well. Before they left here, he, López Rega, was running the household. He was nicknamed "Daniel", and was also known as El Brujo – the Wizard, the Warlock. When Perón came to power again in Argentina, López Rega was given various cabinet posts, including Commissioner General of Police. When Perón died and Isabelita, as elected Vice-President, automatically took over, El Brujo's power and influence became enormous. He embarked on a purge of the Peronist left, including the Montoneros, using a para-police force of death gangs called the Triple A. But he upset the right too. Probably because sensible government, government which would allow the ordinary continuance of business, was impossible with him around. July this year the generals felt strong enough to throw him out – though Isabelita's popularity with the unions left her safe still. He came to Madrid. Was seen here I believe. Then disappeared.' His long fingers fluttered like prehistoric birds, then flopped to his thighs. 'In a nutshell that's José López Rega, known as Daniel and El Brujo. Any questions?'

Silence.

Clemann: 'Thank you, McCabe. Neatly succinct. Señora?'

She shifted on her chair which sighed.

'Yes. Very succinct. And accurate. He was a very strange man. In some ways a buffoon, a fool... but occasionally impressive things happened at his... behest. He had... hypnotic eyes.' She shuddered, looked up, above their heads, then at them, and smiled. 'Since 1968 I was quite intimate with the household, and I met Daniel often. It was therefore natural that he should come to me four months ago. He was frightened. With cause. But he had insurance. He thought. He gave me these tapes, told me to put them in this vault. He paid me a quite large sum. The understanding was that, should anyone ask me if he had given me these tapes, I should say that he had, and say how they were stored here. He hoped this would deter his enemies. I believe he was over-sanguine. I have not seen or heard of him since 3 August this year. I now believe him to be dead.'

Silence. Swivel again. 'Even if he is dead, this does not amount to title to these tapes.'

González delved in a soft leather purse that matched her dress. 'I think this does.' She read from a small piece of notepaper. '"In the event of my death, or in the event of my failure to communicate with the manager of the Velázquez branch of the Bank of the Victory of the Angels on the tenth of two succeeding months, the contents of my deposit box in that bank and control of that box shall pass absolutely and without prejudice to Josefina González, whom the manager of the said bank will identify. Signed, José López Rega, at the bank, and in the presence of the manager and Señora González, this fifteenth day of July, 1975." Now, gentlemen, Señora,' – a slight bow towards Herzer – 'you may dispute the authenticity of this document if you like. But the manager of the bank does not.'

Slowly Clemann tapped one finger on the low arm of his chair. Then he looked up, first at McCabe, then at Roberto.

'Well, gentlemen.'

McCabe cleared his throat again. 'López Rega brought you eight tapes. Five spool-to-spool. Three cassette. And he said these were all recorded by Perón.'

'Yes.'

'Did he bring any other tapes?'

'Yes.'

'What were they?'

'You are going to bid for them?' Before he could answer she shook her head abruptly. 'Yes, Professor, he brought the five other tapes in the box, but as I said before, they have nothing to do with... at any rate they were not recorded by Perón, and they do not concern the present circumstances. As of now they are not for sale. Please forget them.'

No one but Roberto noticed how Gunter's body had gone rigid – like a large cat surprised by an unidentified noise, he was suddenly wary.

'To the point please, McCabe. Do you believe this account of the provenance of the Perón tapes with which we are concerned?'

'If the manager of the bank accepts that piece of paper, then, yes, I accept it.'

Swivel: 'There is still a very large question-mark.'

'Yes?'

'Señora González has unlimited access to this deposit box. OK. Maybe once López Rega's tapes were in it. They don't have to be now. Or others could have been added... '

'That,' said Cockburn, speaking for the first time, 'surely brings us back to the real reason for our presence here. Let us accept González had tapes from López Rega. We can't seriously challenge that. Nor can we challenge the possibility that López Rega had access to tapes recorded by Perón. We are back where we started. All that remains is the authenticity of the tapes she proposes to sell to us. *Let's hear some more tape.*' He emphasised the last sentence.

Clemann: 'Señor Fairrie?'

But Roberto seemed to have drifted into another world: right elbow on the chair arm, cheek supported on his hand, he was staring with fixed, worried intensity at a point in the *Victory of the Angels* slightly above Señora González's gorgeous head.

'Señor Fairrie. Please.'

'Eh? Ah. Yes?'

'What do you think of Señora González's account of the provenance of her tapes?'

The glazed look leaked out of his eyes, then he pulled his body back into the chair, sat upright.

'Yes. I go along with what, er, she has said.' His voice

became firmer. 'Knowing some of the background, the character of López Rega and so on, I am convinced of the provenance of these tapes, that is that Señora González's account of how she came by them is accurate. But their authenticity is still in doubt. López Rega himself might have arranged a forgery.'

'Right,' Clemann sighed. 'Henry, you may give Señora González her money. Señora, we are ready to hear what you have to play us today.' He looked at his watch. 'I fear that the manager will not give us more than another hour, so we had better get on with it.'

21

González chose one of the spool-to-spool tapes and again called on Roberto to set it up. The voice was more vivacious and energetic than on the ones they had heard earlier, more confident, more public, but the quality of the recording was poor: there was background noise, traffic, a bell that tolled the hours and the angelus.

'I got back from Europe at a moment when as usual the political battles were being rigged, the rules fixed to help the oligarchy. The socialists, intellectuals mostly and divorced from the working people they claimed to represent, and the radicals to the right of them, were all determined to maintain legality in the contest for power, and so were hamstrung from the start. I asked myself therefore, what would happen if someone began to fight for real and announced they were going to play to win.

'Nevertheless, my injection of myself into this unclear, turbulent, unresolved situation, was not the unprincipled, opportunist action that many of my detractors have claimed it to be. I had learnt much in Italy, I had seen the way fascism, National Socialism, could be made to work to transform society. I had spent many hours in conversation with *Il Duce*, and some of the greatest thinkers in his movement. I had too seen the dangers, the unprincipled and often unnecessary violence, the often unattractively and unnecessarily brutal way of dealing with the Jewish problem, and so on, and I had already thought deeply on these matters. I do not say that the historic formulations of Justicialismo and the Third Position were already clear in my mind, but they were certainly there. I had a vision for my country, for my continent, for the world even, that motivated quite trivial, or laughable actions. I remember how we pulled President General Rawson to a window of the Casa Rosada and said we'll throw you out if you don't resign. He resigned.'

The voice chuckled, a little huskily, and then resumed its serious but dynamic note. It went on to expound the theory of Justicialismo, the Third Position, the social contract Perón wanted between the classes and the non-aligned position in foreign policy with a wealth of name dropping: Popes, world-famous philosophers, senior statesmen of international repute, all agreed with him. It was all done with conviction and disdain for logic. After ten minutes everyone in the room except Señora González, and Enrico Gunter, who occasionally nodded in wise agreement, and McCabe who continued to make notes, began to fidget.

Then suddenly, at the back of the tape, two female voices could be heard. They were, of course, indistinct, but it seemed one voice was welcoming an unexpected visitor who refused coffee and cakes. González pushed the stop button. 'That,' she said, with a sort of modest glee, 'was me. Isabelita welcomed me and suggested we should have coffee together. But I could see that *El Conductor* felt he was doing well and preferred to go on, so I refused.' She smoothed her skirt. 'Eight, no seven years ago. I was still quite pretty then.' Considering the near magnificence of

119

her beauty now, this seemed a silly thing to say.

Indeed the flow went on, the voice becoming more and more pompous and inarticulate. At one point there was a short break, and clearly everyone could hear the clink of glass and the glug of liquid. Meanwhile, in the bank vault, glances were exchanged, eyes raised in mock horror, yawns suppressed.

Roberto looked slowly and carefully at each of them, trying to make some sort of assessment.

Cockburn he spent least time on. He had his number. A whizz-kid on the skids, seeking desperately to re-establish himself in the media world. The opportunity to present and edit the Perón tapes in newspapers, books, magazines, on TV and radio, across the world, was just what was required. He needed the tapes to be authentic, which was probably why he had been clumsy about setting up scientific voice analysis.

Swivel. Not a pretty sight. Plump. Even fat. Sweating and mopping up with a silk handkerchief. And bored to hell. Has reasonable Spanish, it had been said, but probably not up to unravelling the Voice off the cuff as it were. Well, thought Roberto, he's being paid a fee, and there'll be more fees if Clemann makes an offer for the tapes, but law is not like the media. Law is for real and for ever. The Spanish say no one ever saw a dead donkey or a poor lawyer. He'd like the tapes to be real – still young enough to get a kick out of first-class hotels, first-class flights. But really, he's not bothered.

'Of course the Third Position was one of my greatest contributions to the continued existence of the human race. Oh yes. I know it has been scorned by the Western Bloc and rejected by the Communists. But tell me. Would there have been conferences of the non-aligned nations if I had not made my initiative...?'

120

And Herzer, Becky, she seems withdrawn, intent, preoccupied, has hardly acknowledged my presence. Who is she, anyway? The media person she claims to be? Was she really here yesterday out of curiosity, or is she involved more closely, did she perhaps come *with* Rudel and Adler to hear ... what? That damned second lot of tapes? Roberto shook his head, felt tightness in his throat, a creeping sensation at the back of his neck. She is, after all, German Sudeten by birth and fled the Czech revolution of 1948. And how did she get to be here? Cockburn was surprised, annoyed when she turned up the other day. So did the Señora ask her? Possibly. The more keen potential buyers the better. Yet she remains an enigma. And enigmas frighten me.

'That this concept, the Third Position, solidly based in the philosophical tradition of Justicialismo, was never properly understood was entirely to be expected. Though, of course, at the time, I was too optimistic, too thoroughly convinced of the wisdom of the human race, of the workers – my *decamisados* – of the intellectuals, to realise I stood no chance of persuading the world that I had been granted, *gratia Dei*, a vision of the salvation of civilisation. What I had realised was how deeply implanted pure self-interest is in those of us who lack the gifts of seeing beyond... '

That, thought Roberto, was a shade over the top. And there's that bell again. Have we been listening to this bombast for a full half hour? González, Gunter and Clemann appear to be almost asleep. A moment of fear! Is there proper ventilation? Did the architects envisage so many people shut in the vault for so long? Are we all suffocating? Roberto yawned, and the yawn spread round them.

Gunter, Enrico Gunter. Stocky, solid, well-kept body – probably the Señora finds that very attractive at her age. Beautiful women in their thirties, of uncertain means, don't want penniless, spindly adolescents. They want solidity and experience. And wealth. And Gunter is wealthy. His shoes alone must cost ten thousand pesetas. So what's he doing here? Is he really just doing the Señora a favour, looking after the business side for her, making sure Swivel doesn't pull a fast one? Or is there more to it than that? In arms' manufacture. Astra in Madrid, Beretta in Italy, factories in the Argentine. With a name like that, in that business, he has to be in with people like Rudel and Adler and the Argentinian Nazis. And he really took note when she said those five extra tapes came from López Rega. What the devil are those five extra tapes? Did López Rega really bring them? Are *they* the great attraction, not this Perón *stuff* at all? Gunter frightens me. He can smile, slash with lethal claws, and smile again. His eyes tell you that. And I am frightened because there is more going on here than I know about.

Clemann. An oddity, a freak. His disconcerting height, his withdrawnness, but too his occasional flashes of toughness. When he says 'go', people go, when he says 'come', they come. No doubt seventy million dollars are a consideration, but it's the personality that does it. Mind you, thought Roberto, the personality must owe something to the fortune. It's like the British Queen. You're born to it. Like Juan Carlos ... ? We'll have to see. And he gave a little shudder at the thought of what the next few days would mean. One thing. I am not about to be deported during this period – every policeman of every police force in Spain, and every connected bureaucrat is going to have his hands full elsewhere, once they pull the plugs on that bag of shit in the La Paz clinic...

A buzz near the armoured door and a light above it flashed. Gunter leant forward and tapped the recorder into silence, stood up, went to the intercom by the door, tapped another button. The manager's voice. A customer wanted to use her safe. Everybody out.

They rose, stretched, sighed, grunted – generally the feeling was of relief. Ushered, no, herded up into the main hall of the bank they stood around awkwardly while a small lady dressed very expensively in lace-edged black, chiming and glittering with jewellery, was bowed by the now obsequious manager down the deeply carpeted stairs beneath the chandelier.

Cockburn, already smoking, suggested: 'A countess at least. Checking up her tiara is *in situ*.' He offered González a cigarette.

'Thank you. I prefer my own.' She gestured to Gunter, who flashed a gold case on a level with her very slightly plump tummy. She breathed out smoke – very strong Virginian. 'Actually she is a dowager marquess, and a very good neighbour of mine.'

Cockburn looked mortified, as well he might, thought Roberto. Was he not, had he not too been Pepa's lover, as well as Gunter? And today she was making it very plain that of the two of them she favoured the Argentinian entrepreneur...

STOP.

With hands blue with cold, Roberto lifted the headphones off the close-cropped white hair of his head, pulled the jack from the radio and let Mozart's Requiem, which had followed the Eroica, sound out loud and clear. He rummaged in his clothes suitcase for a second pair of socks, found only dirty ones but pulled them on, padded out again to his icy kitchen. For a time he contemplated the double gas ring and its rubber tube that led to a red gas container. Could he dismantle it all and then get it together in his room without either blowing himself up or losing the use of the gas ring? Probably not. He could move the tape-recorder into the kitchen and turn on the gas where it was. But better not. It smelled, gave off fumes, there was something wrong with the burners. Anyway, in the kitchen he was too near La Aguja... He looked down and across the *patio de luces*, at the window opposite. Still no sign. But that meant nothing. Best of all to put up with the cold and go on giving himself hot drinks.

He waited for the saucepan to boil and remembered how he had stopped listening to all the junk about Justicialismo and had tried to make up his mind about them all. Since then there had been betrayal and two murders. And at least one of them... dear Lord, let it not be Becky. Dear Lord, let it not be Pepa, Pepita.

Tea this time. Coffee could produce a bowel movement. Back, then, to Mozart. At least with the phones on, I can't hear those damned guns and that awful bell.

Sunny morning, now the fog's gone, but not sunny enough to be warm. If no cloud builds up I should get direct sunlight in at about half past ten.

Outside?

Lord. A tank.

Roberto clutched his heart as the spasm of shock and fear surged through his torso. He'd forgotten he'd heard them in the night. Of course they'd be here, behind the Gran Vía, out of sight but ready to move down if necessary. And also they'd be guarding the Telefónica Building itself. No leather jackets, but that means nothing. They're probably on the landing outside the door, the other side of the wardrobe.

No use dwelling on it. Get back to my memoirs, *apologia pro mea vitae*. My cleaned-up slate for posterity. Ha! Only thing to do really until... someone comes. And someone will come. No doubt of that at all. La Aguja. With a bare bodkin. Who is behind him? Who betrayed us?

The jack back in the radio. The headphones on. *Agnus dei qui tollit...*

PLAY AND RECORD:

22

Back in the bank, Cockburn had shown signs of impatience. 'Will we have to go on listening to that crap?' he asked. González looked up at him, her eyes serious but mouth in the slightest way possible pursed as if to push back a smile. Momentarily Roberto felt a terrible nostalgia which he instantly suppressed.

'You would like something a little more... sensational?'

'Christ, yes. Something any publisher in his right mind might want to print.'

'We'll have to see what we can find.'

In spite of the differences in their heights she dominated him.

'Here we go,' breathed Swivel, as the door to the vault sighed open. Then he spluttered, turned dreadfully red as he tried to suppress mirth. Indeed of all of them Clemann alone was not amused or mastered the urge to show it.

The lady, the dowager marquesa had removed every scrap of precious metal and precious stone from her head and body, and even the lace edgings and her mantilla.

González's party again descended into the vault. As they did so McCabe, taking up the rear, remarked from on high: 'I noticed too how there were queues at the grocery stores.'

'Eh?' said Swivel. 'I don't get the connection.'

'Really? You *don't*?' McCabe was incredulous.

'Let us see,' said Señora Josefina González, 'if this will amuse Mr Cockburn.'

This time the voice was intimate again, as it had been on one of the earlier tapes.

'The most beautiful thing in the world. Is a young girl. Mind you, she must be fit, though not excessively so, not like those Russian monsters fed on steroids in the Olympic Games, but properly, as a young woman, a girl on the point of becoming a young woman, should be. With a bloom like that on a peach the day before it should be picked. I remember many girls like that. Mind you Eva was never like that. Not while I knew her. Except perhaps after Doctor Ara had finished with her. Nelly Rivas, however, was exemplary. There were others. I remember Pepita then. She's a fine woman now, make no mistake. But Pepita aged fourteen, playing volley ball with Nelly who was a year or so older. How they rose to the net like swallows! And while Nelly did allow a gentleman of a certain age certain very harmless little liberties, Pepita, who did not, had style. An aloofness. Not that she could not be playful if the mood took her, and would if pressed, offer me harmless caresses. She never let me touch her. And she could fence. God, she could fence. She really could use a foil ... '

CLICK.

This time Pepita González touched the button, not Gunter. Her face was expressionless as she looked up at Cockburn.

'We can do better than that.'

Recrossing his legs, he shrugged.

'I'm sure you can,' he said.

She ran the tape on for several metres.

126

CLICK. The voice still intimate.

'Well. She's back. Upstairs. Mario himself brought her back. He took her away. He brought her back. In a van. With two army jeeps as escort. Thank you, Paco ... '

CLICK.

Señora González pulled the hem of her green dress over her knees and looked around.

'I can,' she said, 'see puzzled faces. Perhaps as we go along Professor McCabe and Señor Fairrie too if necessary will tell the rest of us what it is all about.'

McCabe looked up from his notebook, set as usual on the high platform of his knee. With the hand that held his gold ball-point, he pushed a strand of ginger hair across his freckled scalp.

'Frankly, ma'am, I'm as much in the dark as anyone.'

'Señor Fairrie?'

Roberto shrugged.

'Well then, I'll give you a hint. The date of this tape is 22, possibly 23 September, 1972.'

'Yes.' Recall with the scholarly Professor was at last instant. 'I'm with it now.' He looked around. 'At that time Perón, with a small entourage, was living in a villa in Puerta de Hierra, a select suburb on the north-east boundaries of this city. With him were his third wife María Estela Martínez, known always as Isabel or Isabelita, and several other hangers-on, including López Rega, who, we are asked to believe, is the source of these tapes. At that time intense negotiation was under way to arrange Perón's return to Argentina. Civil war threatened. The Peronists were taking over. All that was needed was the return of *El Lider*.

'On 22 September, Eva's embalmed body was flown from Milan, where it had been buried under a false name, to Madrid. It was delivered in the way the voice we have been listening to has described. There's more background I could go into ... '

Clemann raised a hand. 'That'll do for now, McCabe.' He made a slight gesture towards González, but was interrupted.

'OK. I'm the thick one,' said Swivel. 'But who is Paco?'

Roberto spoke: 'Francisco Franco. He provided the two army jeeps as escort. Perón's gratitude is expressed, I think, with sarcasm.'

'And Mario?'

Roberto looked blank.

McCabe half-raised a couple of fingers. 'That would be Colonel Mario Cabanillas. In 1956, not long after the ouster that sent Perón on his travels, he became director of Army Information. He discovered Eva's body in a box labelled "Radio Equipment". He sent that too on its travels. There's an interesting story in this connection ... '

'Another time, Professor.'

'Surely. But it is a grotesquely interesting story.'

CLICK.

'Upstairs. I really don't know what these people think they are doing to me. Well. They can't know.

'Daniel. El Brujo. Opened the wretched thing. There were five ... six, no, seven of us. Two fucking monks! Who asked them? And the room dark, black, just candles. Why? I can't stand all this mystery, this rubbish. But Isabel, she likes it. Black box, candles at each corner. Of course it was sealed. Tight. With a metal seal. You know the sort of thing. Cunningly arranged so however you fiddled the seal the screws that held the hasps in place were masked. What to do?

'Daniel knew what to do. El Brujo. He went down to the garage below and found a blow torch. One of those things you pump paraffin into under pressure to produce a hot flame. And he melted ... '

128

Jesus,' said Swivel.

CLICK.

'Yes?' González was impatient.

'They're talking about an embalmed body in a coffin?'

'Yes.'

Swivel shook his head slowly. 'They were crazy.'

'Why?'

'Formaldehyde. Ethyl alcohols. Compressed in a possibly airtight box. Quite simply the embalmed body of Evita could have blown them all to kingdom come.'

'Apparently it did not.'

'I'm not sure I want to hear any more of this,' said Herzer, again clasping her hands in front of her to make the odd chopping gesture.

'You can leave if you want to.'

'I'll stay.'

CLICK.

'... the seal. It hissed, spluttered, became incandescent. Dropped away. Well done, Daniel. Paladino opened the box. It needed a lot of self-control on my part to face the next moment. Twenty years... Well. I looked in. That, I said, is Evita. Mind you her nose was squashed, but Doctor Ara who lives here now, has come over since and put that right. Isabel has given the corpse a wash and a hairdo, and my dear sisters-in-law, Evita's sisters, harpies, are here too with a new shroud, the old one having fared less well than the corpse. They want to put her in a tomb here. No chance. The Montoneros and the lefties who call themselves Peronistas want it in Argentina, and that's where it'll have to go.

'Silveyra was there...'

CLICK.

McCabe was brisk. 'Argentinian ambassador to Madrid.'

'And Paladino?'

'Respected politician of the centre-left who was working for Perón's return.'

CLICK.

'... and he told me how she had travelled. It. Asked me to sign a receipt. I did. I had to say something, it was expected. I said: "I spent many happy years with this woman." Ha!'

This time the click was on the tape itself. González let it run and then it came again and the voice.

'They tell me El Brujo has been doing magic. Isabelita lies naked on the coffin and he conjures Evita's spirit into her. As well try to pour a litre of cognac into a half-litre milk bottle.'

CLICK.

'I think,' said González, looking squarely at Cockburn, 'you'll find that printable. In, say, the London *Sunday Times*.'

The buzzer went again. Gunter answered it.

'More clients need access to their strong boxes.'

Clemann unfolded and re-erected himself. 'Tell the manager we'll be finished presently.' He looked down on them all. 'That must surely be enough. McCabe, Fairrie, I don't expect you to give me an answer immediately. Originally I said by two o'clock this afternoon. Now I give you until the same time tomorrow, at the latest. I should add that I expect you to agree on your verdict. When I pay experts for their advice, and they disagree, then clearly one of them is not an expert and does not deserve to be paid. Since I don't know which, neither gets paid.'

McCabe turned to Roberto. 'In that case clearly we must consult. But first I should like to go over my notes.' He looked at the gold watch on his thin freckled wrist. 'Shall we say eight o'clock in my rooms at the Wellington Hotel?'

Clemann instructed Swivel: 'Pay McCabe and Fairrie what we owe them so far. Include a hundred each for their deliberations tonight.'

Three more old ladies dressed in black and jewellery were waiting at the top of the stairs.

23

Clutching his five one-hundred dollar bills in his coat pocket, Roberto walked a block to the next bank, a branch of the Banco Central, where he managed to change them just before it closed. He then entered the Metro at Serrano instead of Velázquez, and possibly for this reason was not followed by a black leather jacket or anyone else. Thus his irritation was all the more sharp when, emerging at José Antonio, he found Cockburn waiting for him at the top of the steps.

'I thought we might have lunch together.' Cockburn took Roberto by the elbow. 'Where do you usually go?'

Not – I would like to buy you a lunch. Roberto, realising they would be going Dutch, said: 'On my own I use a small Galician restaurant near the top of Barco.' It was a lie. On his own he usually bought a snack at an Asturian delicatessen nearby.

'Galician? Not all octopus I hope. I can't take octopus.'

'No *pulpo en su tinto*, I promise you.'

Roberto took the turn by the side of the Telefónica, used Desengaño to cut the corner into Barco.

'Don't you live round here?'

'Very near.'

Cockburn was contemptuous. 'I suppose it's convenient.'

'Very. And cheap. I am not a rich man.'

'So I had really rather begun to gather.'

They turned into Barco – an older street for some of its length than Desengaño. Many of the narrow houses had wrought-iron balconies, and dark bars on the ground floor or in the basement. In the summer the ladies – many of them Blacks or Philippinos, dressed in bright reds and some with fans, sequins and so on – sit on the balconies. In winter you find them in the bars. When they're not working they wear jeans and look like students though fatter and with elaborate ear-rings, and they queue up with the old women in the tiny grocery shops. And that day there were queues. Cockburn almost knocked over an old lady who was carrying two string bags in each hand, all four filled with tins – sardines, mussels in *escabeche*, Asturian *fabado*.

'It's almost as if they expect a war.'

'They do.'

'Do you?' asked Cockburn.

Roberto shrugged.

'And why now?' Cockburn went on. 'I mean the old bandit's been on the machines for a month. The healing process stopped completely ten days ago. But those machines can bleep for a month more if those in charge want them to. So. Why today rather than yesterday? Why today are the duchesses locking their jewels up in the Banco, and the retired whores in Barco stocking up with tins?'

'Turn right here.'

The restaurant was small, clean, and if you got there early enough to be near the stove, warm. If you were not there by two you kept your coat on, which was what Cockburn and Roberto did.

Cockburn ordered spinach broth, Roberto broth with noodles. He knew which would have more nourishment in it. Cockburn ordered *filete*, Roberto hake. It was a long time before they were served. They drank their wine allowance and crumbled their bread away on the damp table-cloth.

'They know,' said Roberto. 'It's really very simple. I mean the duchesses and the housewives.'

'Yes?'

'Tomorrow is 20 November. At dawn on the 20 November in 1936, José Antonio Primo de Rivera, the founder of the Falange, was executed by a legal firing squad in Alicante. The moment is remembered annually by all the Falangists in Spain at dawn ceremonies. They'll declare Franco dead tomorrow morning. Possibly, if he'll co-operate, at exactly the same moment, at dawn.'

'Only one shopping day to Christmas.'

'Precisely.'

Cockburn rolled a pellet of bread until it was grey and compact and then flicked it across the floor.

'Why are they so long about serving us?'

'We are not regulars.'

'I thought you said you came here often.'

Roberto shrugged.

Another pellet of bread was launched into space. It travelled further, into the gravitational field of an Asturian warehouse clerk, who looked up from his copy of *ABC* with disdain.

'I was followed from the bank,' said Cockburn. 'He is sitting at the small table by the kitchen door. Black leather jacket. Funny thing. Swivel, who, believe me, is a creep of the first water, was always convinced he was being followed when we were here before. I think I told you he bought a bullet-proof vest? And we all laughed like drains when he told us. But this time round I think he's right. I wonder why that should be. Ah. At last.'

His broth had eighteen shreds of chopped spinach floating on the surface. In Roberto's there were eighteen small noodles. Neither was hot. Cockburn wanted more to drink, tried to hold the waiter's attention long enough to say so, but failed. The restaurant was very busy.

'I think,' said Roberto, trying to choose his words carefully, 'perhaps more people are in the know this time. Word has got around. Been put around.'

He recalled his street beating, his interview with a Marqués, and the presence of Rudel and Adler at the bank. He shuddered. Perhaps after all it had not been Cockburn's clumsiness in asking *ABC* for a voice sample... for indeed yes, word had got around, had been put around. A top Nazi, 'Evita' had said, was in Madrid, investigating the tapes, co-ordinating a response. Rudel and Adler, at the bank, were part of that response... The sinking feeling returned as Roberto wished, not for the first time, that *he* knew what was going on.

Cockburn leaned forward, waved his soup spoon.

'You could be right. I think Montiam was very discreet. She needed only one rich and unfrightenable buyer to get the ante raised. Really this broth is rather disgusting. And that was enough. But Pepita does seem to have let this lot be known about... I'm thinking of that Gunter chap. Who has he been in touch with?' The thought of Gunter produced a grimace. He looked around. 'I can't say I'm entirely happy with this place.'

Roberto's turn to be apologetic: 'Three courses. With wine. And the present uncertainty has depressed the peseta. It'll hardly cost us a pound sterling each.'

'All the same. So. Interested parties keeping a watch on us. Who?'

Roberto shrugged.

Cockburn pushed back his chair, palms on the table edge, and his eyes widened. 'At least it shows these tapes are being taken seriously. Someone believes they're genuine. Even if you don't.'

'I have not made up my mind yet.'

'But you must lean one way or the other?'

'Perhaps. But I take Clemann's point. I should like to agree with McCabe. And if I find we differ I should like to debate the differences with him until we agree.'

The waiter brought about thirty grams of thinly sliced *biftec*, eight chips, and twenty hard green peas for Cockburn, and the same for Roberto except that a thin slice of hake, bone in, took the place of the meat. Again Cockburn's request for more wine was resisted.

'Clearly,' said Cockburn, after his third mouthful, which left his plate nearly clean, 'you are in need of a bob or two... I won't press the point. You are going to McCabe tonight?'

'This evening.'

'What time will you be finished?'

Again Roberto shrugged.

'Well. I shall be at Pepita's from about nine o'clock. It's two or three blocks from the Wellington. I'd be grateful if you'd drop by when you leave McCabe and let me know the result of your deliberations.'

'Should I not report to Clemann first?'

'Why?'

'He's paying me.'

'You can phone him from Pepita's if you like. That's as much of this place as I can take. I don't want half a stewed pear for the next course. Where can we find a decent drink?'

'The Nebraska in Hortaleza.'

'Come on then.'

He put down notes, did not bother to ask Roberto for his share.

At the Nebraska Cockburn had a toasted cheese and ham sandwich, a coffee and a large brandy. Roberto had just the brandy and the coffee. Leather jacket took a booth four tables away from them. With the warmer and fattier food Cockburn at last drew towards the point.

'Clemann and I are close,' he said. 'Very close. I'll tell you why. We were at Bedales together and thence to Queen's College, Cambridge, both read History, trod the gowns fine, tell the truth, he helped me over an embarrassing entanglement. So, if the tapes are authentic, he'll buy, and he'll set me and Becky up to look after publication. And this is what I have to say, and it is this. When that happens we'd like you to be on board, as our in-house Perón expert. Peter is tight over small things but he likes big things to be done well, so there'll be plenty of money. You get my drift?'

'I suppose so.'

'Of course you do.' He knocked back his brandy, stood up. 'Right then. I'll hear from you tonight when you've seen McCabe. *Chez* Pepita. *Ciao.*'

Leather jacket followed Cockburn. Roberto gave them a minute then followed them out into the street. The cold pinched like a crab.

24

As he turned into Desengaño the Renault 12 with French number plates pulled away from the pavement a hundred yards or so away and came to a halt on the opposite kerb. As the driver's window sank Roberto felt an excitement entirely inappropriate to someone of his age. He could see Becky Herzer's short soft hair lit like a nimbus against the early dusk by the flow of light from the Telefónica.

'Señor Fairrie?'

'Madame Herzer?' Embarrassed he realised that even in those two words he had revealed a little of what he felt.

'You must call me Becky. Can we talk? Do you mind?'

Not wanting to invite her to his awful rooms, where, in any case, she would surely discover things he would not want her to see, Roberto crossed the road, passed behind the twirling exhaust, found the passenger door already open. He got in.

She made no move to set the car going, instead shook a Kaiser loose in its packet, offered it to him. He refused and she lit it for herself. The harsh smoke smote him across the forehead like a blow, and brought nausea with it.

'I think,' she said, 'I should come to the point straightaway. Really, you should declare those tapes to be forgeries. As Clemann says, the whole set-up stinks. And. Even if they are forgeries they are dangerous too.'

He was startled, looked across to her. She was staring straight ahead, with her glasses on, the silk cords looped below her ear. Her hands were clenched tight on the steering wheel, the cigarette clamped between whitened knuckles. Then she turned to him, and said, with a smile that was gentle and even alluring: 'You cannot believe I am here at half past three in the afternoon by accident. I have been trying to make up my mind to come and see you for the last hour or so.'

'I was having lunch with Mr Cockburn.' He paused, went on: 'Believe me he would be surprised, even more surprised than I to hear you say this. He expects you, and I too it seems, to assist him in their publication.'

She shrugged. 'Well, it will cost me to be saying this. It really will. Steve, you, and I could all make a lot of money in this situation. So. Now you will want to know why these tapes should be damned and their publication stopped.'

'Of course.'

She twisted so that her back was almost against her door, put her arm, with the cigarette along the back of the seat. To avoid its fumes Roberto also twisted away so that as near as possible in the small car, they were facing each other.

'You are a socialist. You must realise these tapes will be very damaging to the Peronist movement and therefore to the causes you believe in.'

'Peronismo is no friend to socialism. The reverse.' Roberto was earnest. 'It drew off, still draws off the revolutionary spirit of the Argentine working class and pours it into a leaky bucket.'

'I think you are wrong. I think you are out of touch. What you say was true of the Peronismo of the fifties, of Perón himself, even Evita. But since then it has been appropriated by the revolutionary cadres of Argentinian labour and is the vital ingredient they need to inspire the masses in the struggle that is about to begin.'

'That sounds like opportunism. In any case this is

hardly a judgment you are qualified to make.'

'It is not my judgment.' With a sharp gesture she inhaled smoke, blew it out through her nostrils. 'Señor Fairrie, I am a member of the French CP. I have made reports about your tapes, and have received instructions, arising I believe from consultations between...'

'I don't believe this, I really don't.' Roberto's right hand again searched ineffectually for whatever catch or handle would let him out. Exhaustion, anxiety, the cigarette smoke in the tiny cabin of the car all combined to produce an almost pathological sense of unreality, but too he was conscious of the voices of reason and experience. He really did not believe a word of it.

Herzer twisted back to face the steering wheel, dabbed out the cigarette in a shower of tiny sparks, shifted the gear, revved the idling engine, then let it die. 'Don't go,' she said.

They sat in silence for a time, then: 'You were quite right not to believe a word of what I said. Though I am a Party member. And it is true, very true, that I want your tapes suppressed. That I want to prevent their publication by Clemann and Cockburn.'

'They are not my tapes. Why?'

'It is not now that I think I am going to tell you why.'

He shrugged. She fidgeted, drummed fingers on the wheel. Then she lit another cigarette and smoked it ostentatiously, like Ingrid Bergman or Lauren Bacall in a classic movie, demonstrating tension, creating suspense, perhaps thought Roberto, trying to place the film he had in mind, hinting at duplicity.

'Roberto, I may call you Roberto...?'

'Of course.'

'Forgive me. But I must say this. I sense affinities between us. We have perhaps much in common. We could ... understand each other ... rather well. Your family were well-to-do bourgeois. Yet you are a man of the left. Why?'

A note of sincerity had been struck. Roberto strove to

preserve it, spoke slowly, and simply.

'I hate privilege. Not the privilege of the very rich over people like us, which is not important. But basic privilege. I hate to think that the people who produce the rice, the lentils, the beans I eat may be poorly fed. That the people who made this shirt may not have enough clothes. That the people who mine and process the chemicals and minerals that keep me comfortable may die from enforced overdoses of dust, gases, side-products. That sort of thing.'

Now he felt embarrassed though what he had said was true, perhaps, stripped of theory and rationalisation, for him the only real truth.

Herzer apparently approved. She stubbed out her barely-lit cigarette, and her hand dropped to rest on his knee for a moment.

'I understand,' she said. 'I was born in 1927. In a family, to a background not unlike yours.' She looked at him, head turned, pale brown eyes serious and haunted. 'Solid bourgeois, you know? A small grand piano. Servants we treated like poor relations unless they got puppy... no. Uppish. Both my parents were doctors. Good doctors. They worked for anyone and charged only according to what the patient could afford. Often nothing at all. Of course this was not universally popular...'

She was interrupted. A Municipal Policeman was edging along the pavement recording licence numbers. She restarted the engine.

'Would you mind coming to my place? We could talk more freely there.'

She let out the clutch, swung through the alleyways on to José Antonio, crossed Cibeles into Alcalá. She drove slowly, but very competently, and talked on.

'We were, are Sudeten Germans. Glad, when it happened, to become part of Germany again, whatever we thought of the regime. That did not last. My father was drafted to the Russian Front, not as a doctor but as an orderly. Nothing have we heard of him since. My mother

141

practised a year more, to 1943, then she was ordered to join the medical staff at Birkenau. You know? Under Herr Doctor Mengele? I was fifteen, sixteen years old. My brother was eleven. We were in a home for war orphans. My mother did not know where we were. Whenever she refused to do the things Mengele asked her to do, she was threatened that one day she would find us at Birkenau with her, but on the wrong side of the wire.'

This was all said coldly, recited, like lines repeated too often before.

'After the war she returned to her practice and we were reunited. But although we were liked and respected in what was left of our little community it became clear that Czechoslovakia was no place for us, and we moved, fled, not far, just to Regensburg, in 1948. My mother joined a practice there and our German nationality was established. But I rejected my German past, studied at the Sorbonne, and married a Frenchman. That too is over, but I remain French. Meanwhile my mother has done well, is now much respected in her region, although of course she is by now retired apart from committees and so on . . . '

'Go on.'

'Well. Four times now, this is the fourth time, I have been asked to do things, not difficult or dangerous, or even criminal, but not always to my liking, to protect my mother from exposure and public trial for what she assisted in at Birkenau. This time I have to do what I can to establish that your tapes are forgeries . . . '

'They are not mine.'

'That these tapes are forged. That is all. We are almost there.'

They were off the main road now, threading through narrower streets not far from Las Ventas, the bull-ring. She parked neatly in front of a narrow block, more modern than its neighbours.

But Roberto was not ready to get out.

'Listen,' he said, 'everything you have said indicates... that you were not at the bank yesterday merely to change traveller's cheques. Those German business-men...'

Her head fell forward to rest on her knuckles which still clutched the top of the steering wheel. Then she raised it, shook it, and sighed.

'Of course you are right. But I really was changing my cheques.' She said this firmly and then gave a short laugh. 'But yes, I was asked to be there, first to ask Señora González, Pepa, if I might be there. She agreed.'

Roberto's pulse quickened. 'What did she play? Was it the other cassettes? Not Perón's?'

'No. The same as the first time. The one about Bormann coming to visit. She let it run though. There was something about, oh, I don't know. Money. High finance. Now that really is all there is to say. Perhaps I should take you back to Desengaño. Unless you would like to come up. I should like it if you would.'

'I should like that.'

'Look at me.'

He did. Her eyes were glowing wells of unshed tears, yet they smiled.

'Kiss me.'

'Soon I shall have to go.'

'Yes?'

'To see Professor McCabe at the Wellington Hotel.'

'I know. That's at eight o'clock. It's not quite six. It's not far. I'll take you.'

Her thin brown body pressed warmly into his back, her knees were at the back of his, the delicious difference of her pubic hair nestled near his bottom, the softness of her breasts below his shoulder blades, and her arm curled round his tummy. Kissing surfaces parted, but gently.

Roberto turned on his back, looked up at the coloured glass light-fitting in the form of a bell-shaped flower, that hung above the centre of the small studio flat. As he moved the saggy, put-u-up bed creaked. Their love-making in it had been scarcely competent, comic rather, with a brief shared ecstasy followed by sleep and a waking euphoria which was almost the best part of the whole business. Roberto felt fine. His joints were soft and relaxed and only one thing bothered him. Shortly he would have to wee.

She touched his mouth with a finger, ran it along his trim white moustache.

'And what will you agree with the Herr Professor? That these tapes are forged? I think they are.'

This produced a jerk of irritation.

'Why do you say that? I understand you would like it to be true, but why do you believe it?'

'Well!' She gave a short laugh. 'As Clemann says. The set-up stinks. After the first one.' She was dismissive, swung on her side, her back to him, fumbled for cigarettes.

Gently he got off the awkward bed, glad she was turned from the sight of his sagging bottom and skinny shanks, and crossed the short space to the bathroom. Like the rest of the apartment it was carpeted in brown. Inevitably he left three dark drops, scrubbed at them with toilet paper, made them yet more evident with shreds of tissue.

Back in the room he sat on the edge of the bed, felt the pressure of the tubular frame in his backside.

'Who is threatening your mother?'

She said nothing.

'Who is doing this?'

'Die Spinne, I suppose. You know?'

'And Adler and Rudel are part of the Spider?'

'Part of? No. They are businessmen. Rudel anyway. Adler I'm not so sure of.' She kept her back to him. Smoke hung in layers above her. 'Listen,' she went on. 'The information about Nazis in South America on these tapes may well be accurate. These things can be found out. But if when they are published they are shown to be forgeries, not really recorded by Perón, then no one will believe it...'

Roberto scarcely listened. He was almost overwhelmed with compassion for this thin, brown lady, not so very much younger than he, who had treated him so sweetly. He felt gratitude as fierce as a passion, and guilt too.

He squeezed her shoulder, kneaded it. 'Your mother must be a good woman. A good doctor.'

'I believe so.'

'And what you want is assurance that these tapes are forgeries, and will be revealed as such after publication. I mean, you are not so concerned with stopping publication as that they should eventually be shown to be forged.'

At last she turned. Her eyes were now wary, suspicious, pleading too, but she said nothing.

'Well, really, I can assure you of that. That they are forged.'

He told her exactly why he could be certain that this was the case, and why too, he would still have to try to convince both Clemann and McCabe that they were genuine. She pulled him back into bed, and cajoled him, old and tired though he was, into a longer and more perfect ecstasy than the one before. Then, still with no clothes on so he could continue to enjoy the thin if wrinkled all over brown athleticism of her body, she busied herself about the tiny flat, and produced for him a French omelette with a bottle of Rioja dry white.

25

'I think I should say at the outset,' Roberto said, as he accepted a pleasantly upholstered Oxford chair at a table not so low that you couldn't write on it, 'that I have been subjected to pressure both to declare these tapes forgeries, and to pass them as the real thing.'

'I too.' McCabe took his place opposite. On the table there were the then very few reliable texts on the life of Perón, most of them concentrating on the years up to 1955; also books of reference – the *South American Handbook*, the María Moliner Spanish dictionary, the Larousse English–Spanish, Spanish–English.

'I too,' McCabe repeated. 'And since pressure has come both ways we have really no choice but to give our honest opinion. Not of course that we ever intended to do otherwise.' He leaned back, blinked owlishly through gold-rimmed spectacles over long pale orange fingers clasped beneath his chin. 'Still it puts us in an invidious position. It seems one way or another we have to displease powerful interests. Isn't that so?'

Roberto agreed that it was.

McCabe went on. 'Well, I'll be frank. I am protected. I have tenure in an academic post which pays a quite disgustingly large salary. And I have other connections as well. In short, I don't need money, and I don't think I need fear physical violence. But can you say the same?'

'Certainly not.'

'So, I'm suggesting that since the whole question of the tapes is going to remain unresolved, I would not like to come to a decision, or recommendation on them, that would put you to personal inconvenience, harm, loss.'

Roberto looked back across the table and tried to weigh up McCabe's motives for this apparently considerate offer, and decided that if there was a trap he had better not fall into it.

'That is kind of you. But it is not a consideration at all. Shall we begin?'

'Right. I've drawn up certain headings. I suggest we take each one in turn and see how we go.'

They discussed the sound of the recordings, the voice and delivery of whoever was on the tapes – they were careful never to call him Perón – and the content, for an hour. At the end of it they were broadly in agreement that they had no very good reason for saying the taped voice was not Perón's. But McCabe had serious misgivings which he finally reduced to three or four concrete points.

The quality of the first spool-to-spool tape they had heard was too good since it was supposedly done in Madrid during the same period as the tapes *ABC* had bought. Those, they had been told, had been distorted, there had been background noise, the whole effect was amateurish. And so the sheer professionalism of the recording of that particular tape made it suspect.

'And then,' McCabe went on, 'there is the inconsistency. The second spool-to-spool tape we heard, the one about Justicialismo and so on, did have traffic noise, a church bell . . . '

'How good is good?' Roberto asked. 'I mean are you implying a professional technician was present? That it was done in a studio?'

McCabe deliberated. 'Not necessarily. But certainly someone who knew a bit more than your average home enthusiast, who knew how to position a microphone, get voice levels right. And all the evidence suggests that was beyond Perón.'

Roberto, head twisted away, finally nodded.

'All right. What else?'

'In terms of factual content only one very minor point in the whole lot. The Voice says that Juan Duarte, Eva's brother, should be sent to Martín García for corruption. Now Martín García is, as you know, an island in the Plate estuary, only really used as a prison for political reasons – dictators ousted, leaders of failed coups. It is not a state penitentiary for ordinary criminals. As I say it's a minor point, and since Perón himself spent some time there in October '45 at a very crucial point in his career, it's not perhaps surprising the name came unconsidered to his lips. No. These tapes consistently get facts right. And in a sense that is against them too. Perón was lazy about facts, and what he forgot he made up. That is something you yourself have pointed out. Yes?

'Then again, I was puzzled by what we heard first this morning. All the Justicialismo bit. In the first place it came very close to a section of the earlier tapes, and, as I've said, from the technical point of view it was almost as bad, but not quite to my ear, the same. For instance, there's no church bell near enough to the villa in Puerto de Hierra...'

Roberto had reacted, he couldn't help it. His head swung back and their eyes met across the table. Empty, both refusing to register anything in case either gave something away. McCabe stood up, moved to the curtained window, pulled the drapes slightly apart.

'There are military vehicles parked in the gateway to the Retiro.' He turned back. 'Remarkably similar in style and content to a section of the *ABC* tapes. Why should he record that twice?'

The moment of doubt and emptiness, the moment when pretence had almost given way, was gone.

'Perhaps,' said Roberto, 'he wasn't satisfied with the quality of the recording the first time.'

McCabe came back to the table. 'Personally, I've come to the conclusion that that tape at any rate is a forgery, and a rather hurriedly botched up one. Señora González's intervention, coming for coffee or whatever, indicates she's a party to it. Perhaps the one genuine voice, playing herself, we've so far heard. Finally, I'm not happy about the overall tone of it all.' He drew out the word 'tone' to give it a steady emphasis. 'There is a consistent thread, a common factor that links all we've heard apart from the Justicialismo bit. Perhaps you've spotted it?

'No? Well, it's this. Everything we've yet heard, if published and accepted as authentic, will seriously damage the Perón image and therefore the after life of Peronismo: closer links with Nazis than anyone expected; Evita branded as an incestuous syphilitic by no lesser person than Perón himself; a near confession that he ordered Juancito's murder; his callous treatment of Evita's remains and readiness to use them for political gain, his libidinous liking for pubescent girls... and so on. I just can't quite believe he'd so expose himself. Even to himself.'

'Surely that is why these tapes were kept apart from the others, and not left with Señora Montiam.'

McCabe shrugged. 'That's the line taken by González. And Cockburn.'

'So you really do think Señora González is acting in bad faith. That she knows these tapes are forgeries.'

'Yes.'

'A conspiracy to defraud.'

'To defraud. And to inflict serious damage on Peronismo. Undermine the workers', the *decamisados'* faith in him and Eva. I suspect Cockburn is a party to it. I imagine it was he who pressured you to declare the tapes authentic.'

Roberto said nothing for a time. Then: 'So. Your report to Clemann will say that while you have no firm or conclusive reason for saying these tapes are forged, you have serious misgivings. And you will outline these misgivings in the way you just have to me.'

'That's about it. Now. How about you?'

Roberto took off his glasses, gave them a polish, put them back on. Both frames and vision were still a touch unfamiliar, and he blinked a few times.

'I can go along with some of that, some of the way. However, I think your last point, that the tapes are too overtly damaging to Perón's image, carries no real weight. At least until we know the content of the whole set. I imagine Señora González has been playing the more sensational stuff to stimulate Clemann's and Cockburn's interest. There may be hours of Justicialismo all as boring as what we heard this morning. No one's going to put up two hundred thousand dollars for that sort of stuff — especially when there's already an awful lot of it in what *ABC* and Planeta are going to put out. And I really don't think your other points amount to a great deal.'

McCabe's sandy eyebrows were raised in an expression that was both quizzical and threatening.

'So you think these tapes are authentic after all. I understood you previously to be very sceptical.'

'I still am. But I still have no real reason for saying so. Nor really do you. And there is another possibility we have not considered at all. That some of these tapes are authentic and some are not. Really, to give a soundly based opinion we still need to hear a lot more tape. Don't you agree?'

'Sure. Yes. I'd go along with that. Though Clemann is not going to be pleased.'

For half an hour they worked on an agreed form of words that disguised their lack of unanimity. Then McCabe rang up Clemann.

As he put the receiver down, he said: 'No, he definitely was not pleased. But he will try to arrange for us to hear more tape tomorrow morning. You're to ring him at ten o'clock, and he'll let you know if Señora González will set it up. Would you like a drink before you go?'

McCabe dropped ice from a small fridge into glasses,

added Seagram's. Roberto took an opportunity: 'What exactly was the grotesquely interesting story Clemann would not let you tell this morning?'

'You don't know? Why should you. It was well hushed up. It goes like this. Colonel Cabanillas, you know, who discovered Evita's coffin in a warehouse, was at a loss. To gain time he moved it to the apartment of a Major he felt he could trust.' McCabe warmed to his anecdote, relished it. 'This Major had a wife. Pregnant. The coffin was in the spare bedroom. The Major slept in the living-room with a loaded pistol. In the middle of the night a sheeted figure drifted across the open door and then back. Evita's ghost? The Major thought so, and without pausing to consider what he would achieve by the action, he snatched up his pistol and fired.'

'It was his wife,' said Roberto.

'Precisely. Shot dead. In the head.'

'Not the happiest of tales,' said Roberto, and finished his drink in a gulp.

26

It was about a quarter past nine when Roberto left the Wellington. On the steps of the hotel he reflected, in slightly tipsy amusement (Rioja and a stiff Seagram's) how in one evening he assured first one person that the tapes were forged, and argued very convincingly to another that they were not.

Glancing down Velázquez Roberto could see the line of jeeps huddled under the wall of the Retiro, the black silhouettes of giant cedars behind them, and he remembered how McCabe had admitted to *hearing* the *ABC* tapes, when Clemann had only sent him transcripts. How? When? What did it signify? Clearly, if nothing else, that McCabe was not simply an independent expert, but was playing some game of his own as well.

He turned away, set off up Velázquez, turned right into Jorge Juan, and left into Nuñez de Balboa. On the second corner he was almost knocked down by four tall, lean soldiers in immaculate combat dress with red berets. Paras with battle experience in the Sahara, guns and grenades hung about them, but laughing and clutching parcels of huge *bocadillos* – sandwiches made of whole loaves of French-style bread stuffed with potato omelette. *Santiago y Cierra España* on their shoulder flashes – St James and pull up the drawbridge. Whoever they stayed loyal to would win.

As he walked up Balboa Roberto recalled one of the jokes Ramón had told him. Doña Carmen, Franco's wife, tearful at his bedside, says: 'They are even taking the Sahara away from us.' 'They can't,' says the dying Caudillo. 'I have already given it to Villaverde.' The Marques of Villaverde, Franco's son. Rumours everywhere that as he died the family were plundering what they could before it was too late.

Roberto identified himself through the intercom and the toughened glass door clicked open. Nevertheless the uniformed *conserje* looked up through the window of the *conserjería* and followed his progress across the marble floor to the lift with obvious suspicion. With a fattish oval face and a trim white moustache he looked astonishingly like the already putrefying if not actually dead Generalísimo whose portrait hung on the wall behind him. Roberto shivered as he turned and took in the resemblance before the lift door closed.

A desperate, alcoholic and erotic confusion filled Josefina González's apartment. She was back in black again but this time a shortish dress of crêpe de Chine with a plunging neckline that exposed the inner sides of her small, wide-set breasts; her amber and gold hair was wild, Medusa-like, and her long fingers flickered and sparkled with frenetic agility. Gunter was there as well as Cockburn and both men were not far off drunk. Roberto glanced round, took in each and decided that the problem was that neither of them knew who was to receive the lady's favours that night, and that it was possible that she had not made up her own mind. Momentarily a heavy sadness formed, as solid as a tumour, behind his breast-bone. He accepted a drink from Cockburn who seemed determined to register his claim on Pepa by assuming the role of host. It was a daiquiri – tall, and long, and very strong.

'I wanted champagne tonight,' Pepa cried, 'but do you know there is not a bottle to be had? Extraordinary.'

'Every left-winger in Spain,' said Gunter, 'is waiting

by his TV with a bottle chilling in the fridge.'

'So,' said Cockburn, 'you and McCabe are putting in the boot.'

'The boot?'

'Thumbs down to these tapes.'

'Not at all. But how do you know . . . ?'

'The lady just had Peter on the phone. He was not pleased. He will, he says, pay for you and McCabe to hear one more lot of tapes, then, if no reversal of your misgivings is about to forthcome, he'll piss off back to Genéve.'

'Steve. You must try not to be so boorish. Roberto, I may call you Roberto? Please come and sit here.'

'You may call me Roberto, if I may call you Josefina.' Said with the old world gallantry of an elderly don.

Her green eyes were for a moment warily defensive, then flashed with coquetry.

'I shall be mortified if you do. No one I like calls me Josefina – Pepa or Pepita, please. And perhaps because I like you I shall call you not Roberto, but Papa. Papa Roberto. You are old enough to be my father.'

Roberto realised that she knew she was nearly drunk.

'Now, tell us what has gone wrong.'

The immaculate white hide of the armchair creaked beneath him. He looked up and around at the sunburst clock, the new music centre, a tall vase made out of an incandescent glass, blue like lapis lazuli, and filled with scarlet gladioli flown from Seville.

'Nothing has gone wrong.'

'I should think not.' Enrico Gunter, holding a cigarette just below the tips of his index and middle fingers, drew in smoke, breathed out, gave the tiniest of shrugs – all gestures that seemed oddly effeminate in a man of such solid build. 'I should think not. There are other potential buyers. I personally know of interested parties.'

'Nothing has gone particularly bloody right either.' Cockburn's face flushed darkly, his eyes were almost savagely angry.

154

'Calm yourself, darling, and let papa ... Roberto speak. What has this tall yellow professor got against our tapes? He reminds me of a stick insect.'

Roberto repeated how McCabe suspected the technical soundness of the first spool-to-spool tape and that the one that was badly recorded had been botched up in a hurry to correct that impression; that every extract they had so far heard appeared to damn Perón out of his own mouth in a way which he could not credit. 'That's it in a nutshell.'

Cockburn took it badly. 'Just a moment. Hang about. If he's saying that tape about Justicialismo and so on was put together since Monday, because on Monday Swivel queried the good quality of what we'd heard, he must be implying this was done in response to that. In other words, that one of us who was in my room at the Príncipe that night is party to the fraud.'

Roberto kept his face and voice as bland as he could.

'Precisely. He thinks you and Pepa are in a conspiracy.'

'He thinks *what*? All right, I heard. Jesus. I'll break his fucking neck.'

'Steve. Steven. You really are being boorish tonight. All right. The man's an idiot. How can we persuade him he is wrong? How can we drown these misgivings of his, Roberto, Papa?'

Roberto put down his glass, now almost empty. In spite of the crushed ice he had been drinking through he already felt a warm elation that had dissolved his earlier moment of sadness. He thought: I must not speak or act irresponsibly. Cockburn refilled his glass from a jug, knobbly, decorated, pink – a grand thing but a bad pourer. A splash fell on Roberto's knee.

'I think, Señora...'

'Pepa, please, Papa.' She dabbed at his knee with a tissue taken from a silver dispenser.

'I think... Pepa, you forget my position here. I am,

155

you know, an independent expert like McCabe.'

'But you think my tapes are genuine. Steve, get me a drink please, but weaker than before.'

'I am still open-minded. I must say I was most impressed by your account of their provenance. I cannot doubt any of that. Therefore I must assume that if these tapes are not genuine then it was López Rega who forged them.'

Cockburn stooped over her and his dark eyes tracked down the plunging dress. He set her glass on the marble table. Roberto noticed the beginning of a round belly pushing over the tailored hipster slacks he was wearing.

'Which reminds me, my dear, of what Peter thinks of your account of how you got those tapes. Like Roberto here, he was impressed. Even Swivel couldn't find much to pick holes in. But. Dear Swivel is still not sure, in spite of that document you have, that López Rega will not reappear and claim title after we've paid up.'

Gunter shifted forward. He spoke with finality.

'López Rega won't come back.'

'How can you be so sure?' Cockburn swung to face him, the movement aggressive.

'Because he is dead.'

Pause.

'How can you be so sure?'

The Argentinian businessman placed his broad hands on his spread knees and looked up with a sharkish smile.

'Because a contract to kill was given to the most reliable operator available to those who wished him dead.' He looked at them in turn. 'You don't believe me? Why not?' He pulled a snakeskin wallet from an inside pocket, slipped out a photograph, leant forward and handed it to González. 'Is that El Brujo?'

She took it between finger and thumb. Then paled and choked. 'A handkerchief please, please.'

Cockburn and Roberto pushed handkerchieves at her. Cockburn's was first, Roberto picked up the photo. A flashlit Polaroid of a heavy face with mean lips, parted in what looked like surprise. Eyes, small, open, shocked, sightless. The high dome of a balding forehead was marked by a black hole in the centre from which a tiny dribble of blood had begun to leak before the heart which pumped it, stopped.

'You never told me of this!'

Gunter looked at his squared-off fingernails and again something menacing that yet could be called a smile, twisted his mouth.

'And you did not tell me until this morning that López Rega gave you tapes.'

Gunter sat back in the sofa and silence settled across the room. Distanced by the double glazing and the heavy curtains a police-car sirened down the street.

Cockburn too had lost his high colour. Perhaps out of fright, perhaps because he had reached that level of alcoholic poisoning where the skin goes waxy and one perspires lightly.

'It's not easy... to copy a Polaroid print,' he said. 'I mean – that has every appearance of being the top copy, the actual photograph. Where did you get it? How long have you had it?'

Gunter did not stir. Cockburn went on: 'It's all together a bit much. Contracts to kill. Why kill López once he'd been thrown out? Never mind. Really, I think I'd better get back to Clemann with this. And McCabe.'

He straightened, swayed a little, laughed. 'Poor old Swivel will be scared shitless. He'll be on the next plane back. Contracts to kill.'

'You're not going to stay then.' Pepita held out his handkerchief to him.

'No. Not much bloody use, really. But listen. Can't you find one more bit of tape that will satisfy him? Something straightforward, factual, checkable, and sounding right? McCabe has a point. Too much self-exposure. Psychic flashing. That's a criticism... I am impressed with.

157

But, please, find something Roberto here can be positive about, something that will box McCabe in and make him admit there are no real grounds for doubt.'

'I'll see. I think I can. I must admit I have not yet heard more than half the tapes myself. But I'll do my best. Now. I'll ring for a taxi.'

While she organised his departure Roberto and Gunter sat in silence for a few minutes, then Gunter threw a swift, sidelong glance at Roberto.

'Are you shocked?'

'Even after living for sixty-five years in the twentieth century I am still shocked by murder.'

Gunter shrugged: 'El Brujo killed, ordered the deaths of many. He had it coming to him.'

'But it was not done legally. Or even out of a sense of justice. He must have had many enemies. You have this photograph. Did... did you organise this contract?'

'Or did I borrow it to impress people? Does it matter? Do you think I'll tell you? Listen, a lunatic crook should not hold the positions López Rega held. He had access to too much. Perón himself was discreet. In exile he kept to himself the knowledge he had, did not make the mistake of threatening people with it. If he had, the same would have happened to him. If... the existence of these new tapes, and how they differed from the ones *ABC* bought had been suspected... ' Gunter pouted and shrugged.

'You think they are genuine?'

Gunter's eyes narrowed a little.

'As I say, it was known El Brujo had tapes with him. They disappeared. Here they are. I did not know until today that it was from El Brujo that the Señora got these tapes. All of these tapes. She never told me. Now she has told me... many things will be different. I think.'

'She is in danger then?'

'Not while they are in a bank vault over which she alone has control.'

158

'And if she sells them?'

'Then the danger goes with them.'

Nevertheless, Roberto remained deeply uneasy. *Which tapes was Gunter talking about?* The ones that purported to be Perón's second lot of reminiscences, or the five others López Rega was said to have brought, which, presumably, were not Perón at all?

González came back. The frenetic flamboyance had gone. Violet shadows had appeared round her eyes, her gorgeous hair had begun ever so slightly to droop. She collapsed into her chair again, fumblingly lit a cigarette.

'I should like a Perrier,' she said. 'With ice.'

Gunter stood, busied himself at the drinks cupboard, loped through to the kitchen – a buck asserting his privilege in the place of an ousted rival.

'I think,' – and she let out a long lungful of smoke – 'I should sell those tapes as soon as I can.'

'Yes.' He handed her the water. 'The people you met yesterday will pay for them. But not as much as Clemann might. I doubt if they will go above ten thousand...'

'Ten thousand? But that's...'

'That is what it costs to take out a contract. I know.'

They knew he did. The Polaroid proved it.

She grimaced, hugged herself, looked terribly vulnerable.

'Your people will try to stop me from selling to Clemann.'

'I do not see how they can. The tapes and money change hands in the bank vault.'

'I shall pass on the risk to Clemann and the others.'

'Clemann knows his way around. He can look after himself. Better than you can.'

'But will Clemann buy?' asked Roberto.

Gunter looked at him with curiosity. 'Yes. If you and McCabe tell him to.'

Roberto shrugged, refused yet again to commit himself. He thought furiously. Forget the mysterious second lot of tapes for the moment; remember that Clemann was there to buy Perón's tapes, the dictator's tapes. That was the thing.

Roberto shrugged, refused yet again to commit himself.

Then: 'I too think,' he said, 'McCabe has a point. There is too much in these tapes that is damaging to Perón and Peronismo. No doubt, Señora, you have played only those bits that are most sensational, most likely to catch the appetite of people like Cockburn?'

She frowned, passed a hand across her forehead. 'I think I'm hungry,' she said.

Again Gunter padded towards the kitchen.

'I have not heard all of these tapes. But I would suppose El Brujo concealed only what was most dangerous when they left Madrid, and brought back only what was most saleable when he left Buenos Aires. Amongst what I have not played you is a detailed account of Nazis in Argentina. I cut that tape just as it became interesting.'

'I remember. Go on.'

'Then. There is a detailed, indeed, in a mild playboyish way a rather endearing account of his relations with Nellie. His favourite from the Union of Secondary Students. Apparently she would not go down...'

'All right. What else?'

'A rather witty and amusing account of how a trade union can be subverted, bought, threatened, generally coerced to do what Peronismo demands. I rather liked that bit.'

'And?'

'Let me think. An account of what he knew of Pinochet, of ex-Nazi, German research into torture, of a village in Chile where Nazis develop techniques of repression, interrogation and so on, funded in part by the CIA.'

'So. Most of it, as McCabe says, guaranteed to blacken Perón and Peronismo.'

160

She fixed him with a blank, indecisive gaze. Gunter watched them from the kitchen, sharp knife in hand. 'Yes. If you say so.'

Roberto took off his glasses, polished them.

'And you have heard about half of these tapes, Señora... Pepa?'

She looked at him carefully. 'Yes.'

'Well. I suggest you listen to a lot more tomorrow morning, until you find material that will assist McCabe, and myself, to decide that the apparent bias to improbable self-revelation is not so obvious as it now seems.'

Again she spoke very carefully.

'How long do you think I should spend on that?'

'How should I know? Until one o'clock? Tell Clemann and McCabe to be at the bank at one o'clock. I'll come at about that time. Or... ' He took a chance. 'A little before. I can see myself out. No need for a taxi.'

As he stood up Gunter returned, with a plate of paper thin country ham, a sliced tomato, olives.

27

Roberto was high again as he returned to the street – high on alcohol, fear, exaltation. The momentary exhaustion that had fallen across his shoulders like a load had slipped away again. The night had gone chill, frost glittered on the pavements. Three or four specialist shops glowed like Aladdin's caves, the moon hung above the canyon of the street as if supported there by levitation or a conjuror. He walked a block almost to Alcalá then turned right, listening to the smack of his thin leather soles on the paving, relishing the slight sting that came with it. No one followed. Of all Madrid this part was most like the Buenos Aires he knew, and even after thirty years hankered for – large blocks, stone-faced, built on a ruthless grid system, with expensive shops, restaurants, smart cafés on the street, the offices of top professionals above – lawyers, doctors, dentists – and then huge apartments, like the one his wealthy underwriter father filled with children, an English governess, two other servants, and which his mother who claimed Castilian hidalgo forebears ruled with elegant benevolence.

But Buenos Aires was rarely as crystal clear as this, as clear as Madrid on a smog-free frosty night. Always there had been the presence of a great port, the hint of sea mist between you and the stars, the smell of the ocean. And still to Roberto the stars of the northern hemisphere were wrong, made a pattern strange and untidy.

Four more blocks took him across Velázquez and down the side of the Biblioteca Nacional to the Paseo de Recoletos. He paused for a moment under the trees looking up to the devastation of the Plaza de Colón – skyscrapers, terminals, a vast underground complex of theatres and restaurants now being hewn out of the rock beneath and sweeping away one of the best of Madrid's nineteenth-century squares. From where he stood he could see on the giant boards that masked much of the site new graffiti aerosoled perhaps only minutes before – *Abajo Franco, Amnestía, Poder al Pueblo*, and *Vivan los Reyes*, except this last had been done by an illiterate and read *Biba los Reyes*. There were others too: *JONS*, the Falange sign of yoke and arrows, *Muerte al Rey*, signs of a nation deeply divided. As indeed was his own. As is everybody's in the West.

He crossed the first avenue, stood on the kerb of the dual carriageway as if on the edge of a swollen river. To the right it was a river of red tail lights pouring up through Colón to the northern suburbs, and of white lights coming the other way out of the darkness and into the city. The nearest traffic lights were a block away at Recoletos. He waited for the gap and jaywalked into it. Horns blared and the traffic policewoman up at Colón saw him and her whistle screamed, but he got through, stood panting on the kerb, panting and laughing.

He crossed the east side outer avenue and walked straight into a restaurant bar of a sort he never normally considered. First he used the pay-phone and rang González.

'You understand what I was saying?'
'Yes.'
'It's going to work you know. We're nearly there.'
'I hope so.'
'I always said it would be difficult. And dangerous.'
Pause.

'Where are you now?' she asked. 'Give me the number. I might ring back.'

He did.

She rang off.

He chose a small table still free or just vacated by the enormous expanse of the single-pane plate-glass window that looked back on to the avenue, and ordered a plate of *jamón serrano*, a half bottle of Manzanilla de Sanlúcar de Barrameda, the dryest and lightest of sherries, and a grilled grey mullet. Then he sat back and let his mind dwell expansively and glowingly on what had been done, and what was still to be done. When it came he attacked his thin ham with gusto, relishing its denseness, its darkness, its salty richness, so much better than that of Bayonne or Parma.

By the time the fish was brought, the Manzanilla, not as strong as fortified sherry, but stronger than most table wines, had again sharpened his vision, as if it were mescalin, and he looked about the restaurant with a high happy feeling of camaraderie. Not that the people were those he most approved. There were three or four couples from the quarter he had walked through – doctors perhaps, senior civil servants or traders in oriental carpets in their heavy winter suits, their wives in fur. Three businessmen wrapped up a deal and two colonels ate steak: possibly they were from the Army Ministry just up the road, perhaps they commanded the troops Roberto had seen earlier.

Yet they were the sort of people Roberto had been brought up amongst in the Buenos Aires of the twenties, the sort of people he had married back into in 1940. He could not help feeling at home with them near, could not suppress a warm feeling of familiarity. There was even a priest, a Monsignor judging by the flash of purple on his chest, entertaining with ease and dignity a fine old lady in black, his mother perhaps. He pulled the last flakes from the bone, tidied up his plate, left prongs of fork and blade of knife neatly resting on the plate edge, finished his wine, wiped his mouth and leant back. He anticipated coffee and cognac with pleasure.

Then he looked up and out.

Perhaps he had been prompted by the primitive instinct that we like to believe tells us we are being watched.

Outside the enormous plate-glass window which placed between Roberto and reality the reflections of globe lamps and white-coated waiters moving amongst the Madrid bourgeoisie, stood the fat man who had followed him through the Metro after his second visit to the Bank of the Victory of the Angels.

He was not more than a yard from Roberto. This time he wore a black belted coat with shoulder flaps and a black hat pulled over his small bespectacled eyes, eyes that stared intently at Roberto, met his through the glass, and it was Roberto's that flinched away. A Nazi had hired La Aguja, the Needle. López Rega died from a bullet in the head. Gunter had the photo of López Rega dead, perhaps the proof the customer requires of a contractor that the job has been properly done. Street murder was not the most despicable, not the most horrible means by which the people in this restaurant, the people he had rejected so long ago, maintained, albeit at several removes, their property, their privilege, their hegemony. Was Gunter merely just a part of that amorphous conspiracy, or, as now seemed probable, nearer the sharp end of it?

How had La Aguja known where to find him? He could have been following him all day. To the bank. To the Galician restaurant. To Becky Herzer's tiny flat... Or had Pepita given Gunter the phone number of this restaurant?

The euphoric high did not exactly evaporate – it very definitely changed colour. Roberto rose with dignity, called for his bill, left a large tip and paid at the bar. Good of Clemann to have paid up promptly: at least, thought Roberto, I have spent my last hours in style.

28

'It seemed as good a moment as any to go. I was well fed. That has not always been the case. I was a little drunk – that happens often enough but not on the very best white rum, the very best dry sherry. That day I had made love with a woman. At my age, in my circumstances, I could not expect that to happen again for a long time, if ever. The stars, the moon, the night, the frost. Go on, I said. A bullet now in the back of the neck. I'll even pause *here* and let you do it. *Here*, I recall, was outside the Lottery for the Blind Building. A few weeks ago walking from the Biblioteca I saw two blind ticket sellers returning to base, storming down the street, the one behind with his hand on the shoulder of the one in front, goose-stepping they were, white sticks held high, unsold tickets blowing in the autumn breeze, and as they marched they counted – fifty-five, fifty-six, fifty-seven, LEFT TURN – and faultlessly they marched through the open door of the building. Such courage. Such *élan*. Such a defiant Bronx cheer at the malign universe that had deprived them of sight. So. Remembering them. I stopped at the very same place, wished I had a cigarette to light, but refused the blindfold and waited for four-eyes in the black hat, La Aguja, to end it for me. But he did not.

166

'I walked on. Paused at a small art gallery and peered in at faintly luminous canvases. Stopped at an exotic pet shop where tiny monkeys huddled up to each other in wary, watchful sleep, much disturbed by a nocturnal cousin who swung about a larger cage behind them. Still no bullet. I pushed on to Desengaño.

'Why was I so certain this really was La Aguja? I had looked into his eyes through that restaurant window, through my glasses and through his, and I had seen... emptiness. Not the emptiness one assumes when one knows someone is searching you out, trying to read your mind, the emptiness Pepa and I had once or twice assumed in her apartment, the emptiness that came into McCabe's eyes when he had let slip he had *heard* the first tapes, not merely read transcripts, but the permanent emptiness of the permanently immoral, the emptiness of the eyes of the man who has nothing to hide.

'Since very clearly all concerned knew where I lived, there was no point in going into gross antics to shake him off. At the pet shop window I looked back, and there he was, a hundred metres or so behind. He made no attempt to conceal himself from me, that he was following me. He just stood there on the pavement, legs slightly apart, hands in the pockets of his belted coat. His head shifted slightly and moon or street light lit his glasses, turning them momentarily into ghoul-eyes.

'I pressed on and La Aguja came too down the almost empty streets, but always he kept his distance. In a way it was disappointing – I had made up my mind to it, my mind being high on drink, tolerably good food, and frosty starlit, moonlit night. But I must confess I felt relief too as I slotted my key into the keyhole of our door. I paused. Listened. No feet echoing up the deep well of the staircase, then yes. But they stopped at the second landing, and I heard the bell of the *pensión* peal.

'The landlord is a mean man. He sleeps, but his wife does not. She opened the door on a chain – I heard the conversation. Black Hat wanted a room. She doubted if she had one so late at night, and certainly not if he had a girl with him. Gravely he assured her that he was alone. He passed in his identity card, no doubt wrapped in a five hundred peseta note. She acquiesced and the chain jangled. I moved to our kitchen from which I can look down into the *patio de luces*. A pause. Then a light came on on the floor below ours, on the opposite side of the well, which is a wide one, this being a nineteenth-century building, perhaps its shell is a hundred years older than that. So I could see clearly how she showed him the room, left him. How he shed his black hat, his black coat, then came to the window, put his hands on the sill and looked up at me. Then he turned away and turned out his light. The moon, reflected off his window, concealed whatever he did next, and I turned away too.

'Ramón was not in. And he should have been. The *café-teatro* where he and "Evita" performed had been closed by the police. He had nowhere else to go. Never did he spend the night with "Evita" in "Evita's " flat. It was shared with four other students. When they spent nights together they spent them in Desengaño. So. Where was he? I needed him, I needed him here.'

STOP.

The horrible crescendoing clatter of a helicopter swiftly filled the room until it seemed the walls would burst with the noise. Hands over headphoned ears Roberto watched it come between him and the sun whose first warm caress he had hungrily sought as it fingered its way into his room. Dust and litter, an old nest, whirled away as the monster shifted, swayed, and slowly dropped on to the roof of the. Telefónica Building. Below, a white-helmeted soldier also watched it from the turret of his tank.

The noise leaked away and Roberto returned to his cane chair, pulled flannel dressing-gown closer around him, reached for the buttons, then paused. He pressed the rewind, let it run for five seconds, then pressed the play. His voice sounded dry, squeaky, breathless, tired. He let it run on until the roar of the helicopter again began to fill the room. He made silence, sat and thought. Then sighed very deeply, very heavily, took off his spectacles, rubbed his face and scoured his eyes with his knuckles.

PLAY AND RECORD:

'I think I have blown it, have I not? I am too old, too tired to think straight anymore. Or rather ... to think crooked. I think I might almost pride myself on my failure as a crook, even though the motive was sound. To begin with I told it well – the truth, the right amount of truth, hardly any lies at all. But that was last night. I am sick and old and the best friend a man ever had is dead and still I don't know why, all I know is that whoever killed him must kill me. I should like to think the killers might face some sort of justice. Even Spanish justice. So why not tell the truth, as much of it as I know.

'Barclays International Bank, New York. Pay Roberto Constanza y Fairrie. Ten thousand dollars. Account of J. E. McCabe. And another. Pay Josefina Constanza González. Ten thousand dollars. Considering the payer is blasted apart, and the payee likely to be ... Both payees? Oh God, or, if not God then the dialectical process of historical materialism, spare Pepita. Even if La Aguja is there because of her. She should have told me the truth about Gunter. But we agreed to keep well apart. I'll know soon. Meanwhile, press on ...

'That night, Wednesday night, always hoping Ramón would return while I worked, I started to write a script. Yet another script. It was to be a detailed account of how there had been no hoarding of money or gold or diamonds by either Perón or Evita. Surprisingly enough it started well. Less surprising was the fact that soon I could go no further, I was falling asleep as I wrote. It had been a long day ...

169

Becky! Well. At my age.

'I fell asleep but woke at about three o'clock or just a little after. Perhaps the church bell brought me to...'

He went to the kitchen for coffee and looked out to see if he could make anything of La Aguja. More sober now, the presence of a killer after him seemed unreal, an alcoholic hallucination. The window was black, like a deep pool. He breathed in icy air and thought of champagne, and then he knew. Ramón *was* in Vellas Vistas, in 'Evita's' apartment. The only times he spent the night there were when there were parties – and tonight there would be a party. With champagne.

He had to see him if he was to record this last tape in time. Was La Aguja a problem? No. For three reasons. La Aguja could have killed him already if he was going to. La Aguja could not, from his room, see Roberto leave the building. La Aguja was not La Aguja but a commercial traveller arrived late in Madrid.

29

Coat on again, muffler, black Homburg, still, at night, very much the professional man, Roberto walked down to Gran Vía and hailed a taxi. He gave the road and number of 'Evita's' apartment in Vellas Vistas and sat back amongst the warm odours of cigar and cheap eau-de-Cologne. The cabbie's radio was playing dance music.

'No news yet?'

The cabbie shrugged. 'They'll tell us when they're ready to.'

They passed across the top of the Plaza de España leaving the Príncipe, the Corpus Cristi Bank and the Cervantes monument behind. The wide avenues were now almost empty. Though white-helmeted soldiers and police crouched round clusters of jeeps and armoured cars at major intersections, they were not challenged.

'Historical moment,' offered Roberto.

'Of course.'

Suddenly he wanted to be there. An historian by instinct and education he had often tried to get near the centre at turning-points, nodes in the process.

'Señor?'

'¿Qué?'

'Would you mind? But I think... why not? I think I should like to be at the La Paz clinic. You can take me to Vellas Vistas later.'

'I'll take you as close as they'll let us.'

They took the next major turn to the right and to the east, cut across the north of central Madrid, back to that part of the central artery that was still called Avenida del Generalísimo Franco, and turned north again. Just as the apartment blocks began to give way to villas set in bare frozen gardens, the hospital came into view.

The forecourt was floodlit, there were many more soldiers, Guardia Civil, police. The cabbie pulled his Seat off the carriageway, parked at a point from which they could just see the gates. He turned the radio down but left it still clearly audible, twisted over the back of the front seat and offered Roberto a Ducados. Roberto refused, the cabbie shook one out for himself, snapped a Zippo. Surreptitiously Roberto edged his window down, felt the bitter chill of the air and closed it.

'What time is it?'

The cabbie, a large man, black hair, dark rings round his eyes, gestured with his cigarette at the illuminated clock on the dashboard. Three forty-five.

They sat in silence. The music, distant it seemed, became a wordless tango. Roberto's fingers tapped on his knees and he thought of the Plaza de Mayo in the bright spring sunshine of October – Perón's weather – and he remembered the big bass drums the *lazzaroni* carried and beat in tango rhythms to excite the thrilling energy of the enormous crowds.

Lights behind, down the hill, bounced off the mirrors round the inside of the cab. Three large black cars with motorcycle escort sounding sirens came racing up the wide road from the city, ignoring the traffic signals, moving with power, purpose and disregard for anything that might be in their way, like powerful jets on a radar-controlled flight plan. They slowed only to swing through the high iron gates. Floods brightened and the top of a RTVE camera swung towards them. Silver hair burned above grey suits that shone like silver.

'Ministers. Either it has happened or it is immediately about to happen.' The cabbie stubbed out his cigarette – as a mark of respect?

Orders were shouted, heavy diesel engines coughed into life, tracks rattled and squealed. A line of white-helmeted troops goose-stepped out from an intersecting alley, and, fussed over by a gander-like sergeant, deployed across the forecourt of the hospital.

The cabbie turned up the radio, searched for another station. Still dance music.

'Yet,' he said, 'I'm sure he's gone. It's all over.'

'They'll wait till dawn.'

'Why?'

'To coincide with José Antonio's execution.'

The cabbie lit another cigarette and his fingers drummed nervously on the rim of the steering wheel.

Two military policemen, hung about with guns, grenades, truncheons and whistles came across the road. Roberto wound down the window, said in Spanish but using the German word, 'So. The Führer is dead. Is he not?'

He sensed the deepening of their menace. The larger of them waved, swung a huge fist in front of the windscreen.

'*Lárguense o ya verán.*'

The cabbie turned the key and the engine fired.

'Vellas Vistas?'

'Please.'

He turned right into Avenida del General Perón, followed Roberto's directions across Bravo Murillo into the warren of smaller streets above the university.

'This is it. Please wait.'

The cabbie fiddled with his radio.

Roberto climbed stairs to the apartment 'Evita' shared with other South American students. There was indeed a party, with dope as well as champagne. Ramón was unconscious in 'Evita's' arms. Roberto wrote a note pleading for his presence at Desengaño as soon as possible, pinned it to his shirt and left.

'Listen,' said the cabbie. He had found a French station. There was static but the voice was clear enough. '*Le Général Francisco Franco, Caudillo d'Espagne est mort. Un conseil de regence . . .* '

They drove back to Desengaño in silence. Why? Perhaps neither quite dared to express what he felt – elation? grief? fear? hope? – in case it would not be shared by the other. Roberto paid off the cabbie with pesetas changed from Swivel's fistful of dollars, and got back into his flat, for the second time that night, without being pounced on by La Aguja.

He was now entirely ready to dismiss the fat man who had followed him from the restaurant near Colón as . . . just a fat man. A commercial traveller perhaps, arrived in Madrid late at night, perhaps from Barajas or the Chamartín railway terminal, coming from the Recoletos subway railway station, looking in at a restaurant too expensive, and then wandering into central Madrid looking for a cheap *pensión*. As he slopped brandy into a tall glass he accepted that high as he had been on alcohol, exhaustion, excitement, and Gunter's Polaroid photograph of the murdered López Rega, he had been too ready to believe what now seemed palpable nonsense.

At his desk he pulled paper towards him, set his glass at his side, switched on the radio which still played wordless light music and, with the electric fire between his feet, began to write.

There had been (and it seemed the ghost of Perón stood behind his shoulder and gave dictation) no hoarding of money, gold or gems by either Juan Domingo or Eva. Oh yes, he engagingly admitted, a certain rechannelling of state funds, and yes, there had been personal extravagance. There had too been lavish generosity – to friends, family, supporters, but also to the poor, the needy, the underprivileged who had been so remarkably championed by Eva,

174

and so scandalously neglected since 1955.

But no massive movement of funds to Swiss banks, no hoards of gems smuggled abroad in the false bottoms of suitcases.

It was a creative flow, Roberto scribbled as if possessed. He had felt the possibility before, had distrusted it, rejected it. But now... why not? For thirty years Perón – plump, jolly, toothy (at first they called him Colonel Kolynos, after the toothpaste) – had been there in his life. Three years of hope and trust, two of hope, and twenty-five years of hate, confusion, and now, lately, a sort of understanding. Trying to get the tapes right he had learnt even a sort of affection for the charlatan, the rogue. Not a mass murderer (how could he be when his central power base was the masses?), a physical coward, perhaps, who certainly side-stepped and lost whenever he was faced with violence, he had been no Pinochet, no Nixon, no Kissinger.

And now, prompted by the necessity of producing a tape McCabe would unhesitatingly accept as genuine on all counts, he wrote as Perón would have wished it, recreating a Perón more like what Perón wanted to be than ever Perón himself had achieved on the *ABC* tapes.

At six in the morning the dance music stopped and the regular first newscast of the day began. Incredulously, flooded suddenly with weary despair, Roberto heard that the Caudillo, though worsening, was still alive. Other items followed. Then silence. Then the Minister for Information was announced, and at last it was official. Spain was allowed to know what the rest of Europe had known for two hours. Franco was dead.

Roberto raised his glass, drained it, and rolled, still dressed, into his narrow bed, and slept, again.

30

He awoke at ten and panicked. At ten he was meant to phone Clemann. There was still no sign of Ramón, he had not finished his script, there was no chance of getting the new tape to the bank before one o'clock. Clearly he had to make contact with Pepita, though the agreement was that this should never be done unless there was an emergency. Any evidence of collusion between them, however slight, would be the end of everything. But this surely was an emergency.

Roberto pulled on his outdoor clothes, found a handful of pesetas for the public phone boxes, and slithered and clattered down the stairs past the *pensión* entrance and out into the street. He hardly gave a thought to the paranoid delusions he had entertained about the traveller, no doubt Galician, who had arrived behind him the night before.

Outside the José Antonio Metro each of the phone boxes had a queue of at least two people. As he joined one of them the user, a large working man in donkey jacket and jeans burst out, swearing – nothing but engaged tones and crossed lines. The lady in front of Roberto shrugged – 'The Caudillo is dead,' she said. 'The whole world phones Madrid, and everyone in Madrid tries to phone everyone else.' She turned away and Roberto took her place. It was all true. He replaced the useless handset, scooped up his returned pesetas, thought of the Metro, rejected it, sighted a miraculously empty taxi and flagged it down.

He had time now to take in the city on the morning of Franco's death. It was, as the bulletins said, calm, and, with the news still little more than four hours old, unchanged. Shops and, Roberto noticed with despair, banks were open.

Outside Pepita's apartment block he pressed the buzzer three times, got no answer, and at last resorted to the keys she had given him but told him never to use unless the success of their scheme was under terminal threat.

The *conserje* had draped the portrait of Franco with black.

The locks in Pepita's door opened almost soundlessly, and as he let himself in he heard her cry – a moan, a sob, a gasp, something of all three, and then repeated, once twice, rhythmically. He was standing in a tiny hall off which three doors opened – the living-room, bathroom, and bedroom. The bedroom door was ajar. Two steps only took him to the gap. It was not a room he had ever looked in before. There was a small bright chandelier, a lot of quilted leather and yellow quilted satin, and many mirrors. He took it all in in less than five seconds and the images he left with were confused but vivid.

Pepita was kneeling on the bed, her body very white in contrast to the yellowish gold of Gunter's. He was standing behind her thrusting at her from behind.

Roberto fled – out of the door, ignored the lift, stumbled down three flights, across the marble hall, out into the cold bright air. He leant against the bronze door jamb and heaved and coughed, even let his knees sink a little before pulling himself together sufficiently to stagger down and across the street to a bar where he drank, because he could not think of anything else to ask for, coffee and brandy.

Twenty minutes later he went back to the street door and again pressed Pepita's buzzer. This time she answered, said she would join him in the bar as soon as she could.

'You came in an hour ago. You saw.'

'Yes.'

She was in her sable, her hair was wild, thrown up like a mane above her forehead, her face white but bruised on the left cheekbone. Her top lip was swollen. Roberto longed to take her in his arms, comfort and caress her into some sort of quietness. She shook out a cigarette, lit it.

'I think he saw you. In the mirror.'

'So?'

She shrugged. 'I don't suppose it matters. Too much. He knows... suspects or has guessed what there is to be known. Why did you come?'

Her anger was manifest – he sensed she wore it like a mask to cover... what? Shame. Humiliation. He wanted to tell her that it did not matter that he had seen what he had seen, but he could not.

'I can't get a new tape to you by one o'clock. Ramón is up at Vellas Vistas with "Evita". Lord knows when he'll come back. Lord knows if he'll be in a fit state to do anything when he does come back.'

She stirred sugar into her espresso, flung back her head and her angry green eyes glittered at him.

'It doesn't matter. It doesn't matter at all.'

'Why not?'

'Listen. Haven't you heard the bulletins? Don't you know what's happening?'

'Not since six o'clock this morning.'

'Three days, full mourning. He lies in state from tomorrow morning through to the funeral on Sunday. The King will be sworn in at the Cortes on Saturday. The banks are due to close at any time and will not open again until Monday. You've got four days. Four whole days.'

'But Clemann... ?'

'Clemann can't get in touch with me, nor I with him by phone. They are jammed, or I can pretend mine is. He won't seek me out in person. Nor even send Steve. That would be a sign of weakness. So. He'll sit it out until I ring him. Anyway,' – she gestured a little wildly and gold chains chimed and flashed as they slipped down her thin veinous He can't leave.' She drew in smoke, breathed it out through He can't leave.' She drew in smoke, breathed it out throuth flared nostrils like a dragon. 'The question is. Can you get together a tape that really will answer that orange lizard's bizarre objections?'

Roberto remembered the creative flow, the sense of Perón himself giving dictator's dictation at his ear.

'Yes.'

'Well then. That's fine.' She shrugged the sable about her, drained her coffee, stubbed out the cigarette, pressed a precise finger and thumb into the corners of her mouth. 'His lordship thinks I have gone out for eggs. I had, I suppose, better find some. Somewhere. Oh yes. Last night. After you phoned me from that restaurant at Recoletos he asked me who had rung and where from. He had seen me take down the number. I told him.' She touched her bruised cheek. 'Why not? Then he rang someone else. Called Betelmann. Who is he?'

Fear and despair rose like vomit.

'He is,' said Roberto, 'sometimes known as La Aguja, the Needle. Probably he killed López Rega...'

Her anger dissolved. Her face dropped into her hands and she sobbed. He came round the table, put an arm round her, and twisted his fingers into hers.

'Oh Papa, Papa,' she moaned.

'Pepita. *Querida*,' he offered. 'I always said it would be difficult. Dangerous. I always said so.'

Nevertheless as he strode through the chill streets back to Desengaño he found her breakdown, her tears not quite convincing. Or rather, though genuine enough – she really would be sorry if he came to harm, he was sure of that – he felt that in her scheme of things he was not the most important thing of all. Before his skin she would certainly put her own; for less, for certain luxury and security, she might well sacrifice him. She was, after all, part of *them*, part of the corrupt conspiracy of the rich and the would-be rich; she lived off and at the mercy of people like Gunter. In short, he did not believe that it had been absolutely impossible for her to withhold the restaurant phone number from her Argentinian lover.

Obeying the traffic lights he began the crossing of the Paseo del Prado at Cibeles, and in the middle found himself caught in a jostling but silent and surly queue that was forming round the kiosks. The first papers printed since the announcement of Franco's death had appeared on the streets. He allowed himself to be pushed forward to the vendor, found there was as yet no new edition of the new liberal paper *El País*, to avoid argument bought the popular *Ya*.

Scarcely bothering to look at it he hurried on. The giant electric clock and thermometer above the junction of Gran Vía and Alcalá registered 3° and 11.55. He was surprised. It felt colder. And then he saw a man banging helplessly on the glass door of the Banco Hispano Americano, and he realised with a touch of panic, that Pepita had been right – all round him shops, businesses, banks were closing, shutters going up. Had he enough food? Enough money? Yes, of course. He certainly had enough money.

He shrugged. There were always wine, brandy, coffee and tinned sardines at Desengaño.

He walked the last couple of hundred metres more slowly and brought himself to face one of the questions he had been avoiding. What was Gunter up to? *No sé*. I don't know. Gunter had known Pepita for many months. As far as the tapes were concerned Roberto had no reason to suppose that Gunter thought of them as anything but genuine. *Unless Pepita had told him otherwise*. The man was a bully, a moral degenerate, a fascist. He was also rich and unscrupulous. Why had he sent La Aguja to follow him to

180

Desengaño, to take a room from which he could watch Roberto's attic? Because, in spite of whatever Pepa had told Gunter, Gunter believed there was still more to know.

There was some comfort in this thought. As long as Roberto knew something (though Lord knew what!) that Gunter wanted to know, then presumably his skin was reasonably likely to stay whole. At least as far as La Aguja was concerned. And meanwhile there was still just a chance that a sale could still be agreed with Clemann. The danger would pass with the tapes to him — and they might yet make the sort of money they hoped for.

Roberto laboured through the later afternoon and as he did, the script became sluggish, nasty, dead. No longer did Juan Domingo Perón strut about the room behind him, no longer did he feel the power all but the most self-denying historians feel as they mould and shape the clay of fact into the subtle pottery that those who pay them will accept as true.

His mind was poisoned. By fear: the fat commercial traveller who rented a room below his own and across the *patio de luces* dealt after all in death; by the wretchedness of knowing that Pepita would never quite forgive him for having actually seen her at her trade. By guilt: he had promised Herzer he would expose his tapes once Pepita had sold them — now he doubted he would have the courage to do so. By guilt again: if he did not expose them he would have put lies on the market and profited from them. I am, he thought, an old-fashioned bourgeois at heart — my word is my bond.

Not long after darkness fell there was a knock on the door — knuckles against the whitened patch where the Sacred Heart had once been nailed. He peered into the ineffective spyglass and saw McCabe. Terror subsided. It could have been Betelmann, La Aguja, the Needle.

31

'May I come in?' McCabe did not wait for an answer but stepped forward. Roberto moved to avoid the humiliation of being pushed.

He panicked. There was nowhere to put the tall gangly American except the kitchen or bathroom, nowhere, that is, where there was not evidence of some sort or other that the apartment was a factory for the production of Perón tapes. He tried to shepherd him into the kitchen.

'I'm afraid we're rather unorganised.'

'So I see.'

McCabe stood in the doorway, his thinning gingery hair almost touching the lintel. He surveyed the filthy cooker, the crowded sink, the narrow white-topped table stained with rings of dried red wine. 'You must have a living-room.'

He turned up the short narrow passage.

'The further one.' Roberto indicated his own room with a sinking feeling that all was now lost. 'More a bed-sit really.'

He pulled himself together, made a last effort, drew on resources provided by an English public school, albeit progressive, and Cambridge.

'I say, you know. I do think you've got a nerve. Barging in like this.'

'Really?' McCabe folded himself down on to the cane

chair, looked around slowly, nodded to himself. 'Really!' He mimicked Roberto's Englishness back at him. 'I say, be a fine fellow and get us a cup of coffee, and we'll talk it all over, shall we? Black. One sugar.'

Humiliation continued. Roberto, agitated, found he could not unscrew the top section of the espresso coffee maker, and there was no Nescafé. He had to take the pot in to McCabe who twisted it apart with ease, in spite of the thinness of his wrists and fingers.

Worse was to come. When the coffee was made and he carried it through McCabe was, of course, reading the script Roberto had been composing. He glanced sideways as Roberto placed the coffee at his elbow.

'I have to say,' he said, 'I rumbled Josefina Constanza González quite early on. Who, incidentally, I take to be your daughter. Yes?'

Blankly Roberto assented.

'But I didn't too quickly see how you fitted into the act. Clearly these tapes were forgeries. So the lady had to be fronting for someone.'

Chagrin bit. 'Clearly?'

'Oh, don't misunderstand me. The quality of the performance is exemplary. It might not get by an electronic analysis, but then that's not going to be that easy to set up. And it's a game lawyers and experts love to play. They could keep the thing going for a year or more, cost a million.

'Content-wise there are problems – but nothing insurmountable. Mainly, as I said last night, they're too anti-Perón. That guy wore a mask all the time. He never let it drop. Not even to himself. And now I see you are attempting to adjust that bias.' He tapped Roberto's script. 'The actor of course is Ramón Puig.'

To deny this too seemed futile.

'He's very good. You see, when I came over to help *ABC* with the real tapes, I saw that poster' – he pointed to it on the wall: *Los Peroles* – 'and of course I had to go along and see it. Great. I liked the script. But Puig *was* Perón, and that Castillo as Evita was something else again. But that's by the way. I had no reason to make connections then and your name did not appear in the publicity. No. The first reason for suspicion was the whole set-up, the ambiance of it all. It was too like a re-run of the Montiam episode. And then I have my contacts in the Perón household too, you know? And they were as certain as could be the Montiam tapes were the only ones Perón made. And so on. As for you, I began to ask myself and others questions about you the second time I saw you set up a tape-recorder. The first time you were a bumbling old fool who did not even know where the flex was housed. The second time you ran it like a disc jockey. Well. I'm in touch with resources, databanks and so on. You have left-wing affiliations for half a century you acquire a file or two, you know?'

He finished his coffee.

'I've still not figured how you got in on the act up front as a Perón expert in Clemann's pay. I guess it was through Cockburn, but I don't think he's in this with you.'

'He is not. Early on, six months ago, I wrote to him saying I was an expert on Perón and Peronismo with a book I wanted to publish. He came to think of me as an independent expert who happened to live in Madrid.'

'Neat. In fact all in all it's been quite a neat little operation. The question is, where do we go from here?'

'Yes. Indeed.'

Silence lengthened between them.

McCabe pushed out his long tweedy legs, folded his fingers together under his chin.

'Whoever,' he said, 'acquires these tapes of yours will, in one way or another publish them in an edited version. The point is to what end will the editing take place?'

'But if you say they are forgeries, who will want them?'

'Come on. Any buyer, Clemann or anyone else who actually buys them, will find experts to say they are good.

You know that. To what end the editing. Clemann would cut out repetition and ennui. He would not respect certain perfectly legitimate interests that could be inconvenienced, at the very least, by publication. That would not be a consideration for him. And I think it should be. It is not only legitimate, it is essential, *pro bono publico*, that responsible persons, with clear guide-lines, should handle material as sensitive as this... '

'You go on talking as if the tapes were genuine.'

'Saleable. Which is genuine, real. Definition of reality – you can exchange it. So. I conceive it as a responsibility to make sure these tapes do not fall into Clemann's hands, that they should be properly... sanitised before going out into the market-place. In point of fact it is not merely a responsibility. It is in this case a commission.'

'I don't follow you.'

'Well, we'll see. Is there any more coffee?'

Roberto reheated what was left in the pot, and in the kitchen remembered La Aguja. Was he still sitting on the floor below, across the well, looking up at the lights in Roberto's apartment? He shuddered, stared at the frosted glass of the closed window with a sort of fascinated revulsion, then turned away. He took the pot back into his room, refilled McCabe's cup, set the pot on the table at his elbow.

McCabe drank, dabbed his lips on a large blue handkerchief.

'Just let us continue to temporarily hypothesise that your tapes are genuine. As I say, if that were the case, I would have been commissioned to make sure they fall into responsible hands.'

'Whose?'

McCabe made an odd little pout – half grin, half grimace. 'Those of the Great and the Good. Whose else? Whose servant I am. As the one politically reliable, academically accredited expert in a very important area of Latin American studies, I naturally do not withhold my services when

185

the State Department asks for them.'

'Clemann knows nothing of this.'

'No.'

'And he employed you before?'

'Indeed yes.'

'And sent you transcripts of the Montiam tapes?'

'Yes.'

'And later you *heard* those tapes. You admitted as much.'

'That's right. Once *ABC* had them I got to hear the lot.'

'Assisting them in the process of sanitisation.'

McCabe shrugged. If he was on the defensive at this point he hardly showed it. 'That was perhaps the idea. It was scarcely necessary. There was very little of interest in them. They were boring and repetitive. And downright inaccurate. They were the almost mindless wanderings of an old man rewriting history to justify the mess he'd made of it when he was in a position to do so. Let me tell you, Fairrie, your tapes are a heck of a lot more interesting. I'll come to the point. I want to buy them.'

'Oh dear Lord.' Roberto struggled to his feet, pushed across the table at the window catch, knocked the espresso pot so it fell across his papers spilling a dribble of grainy brown, got the window open. A gust of freezing smog blew in on them, and the subdued traffic noise from Gran Vía. Then he shut it again, subsided back on to the bed. The room was very small, and he had to twist his knees away from McCabe's to avoid contact. 'Why?'

McCabe was brisk now. 'They are like a palimpsest. Under layers of other stuff they actually do contain real information that is not available elsewhere. You had your sources close to Perón, like Señora González who no doubt gave you the details of how the old lecher carried on with his nymphets. Then there is the stuff about Nazis and their immigration into Argentina. Martin Bormann is alive and well...'

'You weren't there when that bit was played.'

'You can be sure I heard of it.'

Who from? Roberto struggled to disentangle the web of possibilities.

'And checking back it was accurate, very accurate. Source?'

'A friend of "Evita's". Castillo's. Another Montonero. He came from a family that had married... been married into by... *émigrés*. I never met him. They judged it would be safer if I did not. Ramón and "Evita" came home with the facts, and I wrote them up.'

'Do you mind telling me just about when did this source of information materialise?'

'Why should I mind? July this year. Early August.'

McCabe nodded slowly, owlishly wise.

'You see? I really do think your tapes have real value. And I, or Milton University, Iowa, which I represent, is, are, ready to... to take them off your hands.'

Roberto was now deeply confused. Not least because McCabe had guessed quite wrong where Pepita was concerned. The bits about Perón and his nymphets, including Pepita, had all been invented by Roberto. For all the *demi-mondaine* aspects of Pepa's lifestyle, she had been brought up an ultra-Catholic in an ultra-bourgeois (once Roberto had left it) household. It was unthinkable that she should talk to her *father* about such things. And now, educated twentieth-century man that he was, he guessed he had projected his own desires concerning his daughter on to Perón, who was, of course, a father figure... Stop. That way madness lies. Or sanity.

He was shocked too, in spite of himself, at the duplicity of this academic, this representative of the liberal, humanist tradition, the tradition that had created such fine and independent temples to science and the arts as Milton University, Iowa.

All he could think of saying, after a long pause was: 'What, if we sell, will you do with them?'

'They will go into Milton University archives as the real thing. With my say-so pinned to them there will be no questioning of their authenticity, no way will an electronic test be thought necessary.' There was an appeal here to Roberto's vanity. 'It will be announced that they will be a major source for a definitive biography that I am working towards.

'Meanwhile, however, they will be available to other researchers, and even the media, as and when the other people I work with see fit.'

'The State Department.'

McCabe assented. Was there something again almost coy in this admission? If so, why? Was he checking a tendency to show pride in his connection with real power? Or was there a residue of guilt that he thus compromised the always dubious independence of Academe? Perhaps an uneasy mix of the two.

'Sure. The State Department.'

'And what criteria will determine how they use the tapes?'

'What do *you* think? They will use them, quite rightly in my view, according as to how they will perceive, in the constantly dynamic situation that always pertains in Latin America, they may best assist the execution of State Department policies in that area, at any given time.'

Roberto took breath. 'You cannot imagine it was ever any part of my design that they should serve the interests of the State Department.'

'No. I cannot say I imagine that. But. You and the State Department do have a lot in common. A deep dislike of Peronismo. To that extent your tapes will be in good hands.'

It could have been a cry of pain, but it came out like a squawk: 'Doctor Kissinger's!'

Again the coy shrug. Roberto guessed that McCabe

rather liked the idea of Kissinger – the academic who'd made it so far outside Academe that he could drop bombs on a genocidal scale.

'I have to think about all this.'

McCabe looked at his watch. 'Five minutes. Right?'

In his squalid kitchen Roberto drank brandy and tried to arrange his thoughts – and all, finally, he could think of was the danger, and the money, and then again the danger. Ramón and Pepita remained at risk while the tapes were in Pepita's possession. All very well to knock the liberal humanist stance – but this was his daughter, his only child, and the other his best friend. It was time to call it off. They had intruded themselves into a thoroughly nasty world – children floating paper boats amongst crocodiles. Perhaps there was still time to paddle back to the edge.

'How much?'

'A hundred grand. Dollars.'

'Ramón and Pepita may not agree.'

McCabe said nothing. Roberto pushed on: 'I think a deposit would help. Ten thousand dollars for each of us.'

McCabe pulled out a cheque book, wrote, tore off, went through the action three times.

'You have dated them the twenty-fifth. Tuesday.'

'That's right. Earnest of my good intentions. You get the rest in cash, Monday, at the bank, at two o'clock precisely, where and when you hand over the tapes to me. But if you don't come across, these cheques will be stopped. I'll leave it to you to make sure González gets it all properly set up. I'll see myself down.'

He unfolded himself, reconstructed his spindly height, reassumed his herring-bone tweed top-coat, brown scarf, leather gloves. He took his hat, which exactly matched his coat, and said: 'Perhaps too you'll consider an option on the next instalment?'

'I don't follow you.'

189

'I mean, we might want to give you a scenario for some more tape. You and Puig could then . . . ?'

Roberto was suddenly very angry, but he concealed it. 'I don't think so.'

McCabe shrugged. 'Think about it. Oh. And by the way. I want all the tapes. All thirteen of them. Is that understood?'

'Thirteen?'

'The eight, no nine, you made, so it is fourteen *in toto*, and the five you did not make.'

Roberto opened the door, standing aside as he did so. It was as well he did. One bullet at least passed right through McCabe, and ended up in the ceiling. The body was thrown against the door jamb, but then toppled forward, loose limbs at last definitively unhinged, down the narrow flight of stairs towards where his killer had stood.

32

'Ramón came back an hour after McCabe was shot. Before I could tell him about that, he told me that a man in a leather jacket was standing on the landing below ours. Ramón was not in good shape after twenty-four hours of champagne and dope, and was in worse shape after I had told him that a murder had been committed on our door-step. The body had been taken away of course. Blood and things nastier wiped up, by, I rather think, the Galician landlady downstairs. Not long after the noises of swabbing and so on I saw her from my kitchen cleaning out a bucket in hers. There was no sign of La Aguja, but that meant nothing.

'For an hour we debated what was to be done, and concluded we could do nothing. Neither of us was ready to go out into the streets, not even as far as a call-box, in the middle of the night. Neither of us was ready to go to bed. Ramón told me of demonstrations near Vellas Vistas, of Falangists returning from the dawn ceremony at the tomb of José Antonio in the Valley of the Fallen, where Franco will shortly be put, returning and chanting *Muerte al Rey*. Others, or the same, had cheered Pinochet's arrival at Barajas, thus signalling support for any Spanish general who might be making up his mind to do to Juan Carlos

191

what Pinochet did to Allende. He showed me a PCE leaflet urging the workers to strike, to form soviets, to march on the prisons and begin the final battle for democracy.

'Definitely there were plenty of reasons for staying indoors. I have experienced similar situations in Barcelona in 1936, and in Buenos Aires. All street murders are deemed to be political and none is investigated. People settle scores.

'Neither of us wanted to sleep, but in the end we had to. In bed I tried to forget McCabe's body smashed with heavy bullets, tried to remember Becky's warmth and tenderness the day before but that pleasure was vitiated by the stupid promise I had made her. Bone and blood splattered across the door intervened, and in the end I had to take some of Ramón's Seconal.

'At dawn or not long after we listened to the radio. The night had been quiet and Franco's body was already in the Palace. We drank coffee, wondered again what was to be done. I explained to Ramón that we had already made ten thousand dollars each, showed him McCabe's cheques, and argued that for the sake of our own safety, and Pepita's, we should call it a day, hand the tapes over to whomever wanted them, and explain they were forgeries. Get back to terra firma before the crocodiles snapped again.

'He shrugged, said an odd thing: "Not bad pay really, since, when all was said and done you and I were little more than bait."

'How to get out without being murdered or kidnapped, how to get to Pepita or Clemann was the problem. Intermittently we listened to the radio and it provided an answer. An enormous queue was forming to view the cadaver, already it stretched up Bailén and into Plaza de España. People were advised to approach its tail via José Antonio, Gran Vía. Ramón insisted that the fascist propaganda machine was exaggerating the numbers, but looking out of the window and into the street we could see a steady flow of say ten at any one time of people in mourning moving towards Gran Vía. If there were so many in Desengaño, there must truly be a vast crowd coalescing in Gran Vía.

'Ramón's Thespian instinct asserted itself. He insisted I should dress the part. While I searched out clean linen and black tie he brushed my suit and cleaned my shoes. Soon I looked the very model of a modern bourgeois gentleman in mourning.

'Bravely he went ahead of me down the stairs and shortly I heard him asking leather jacket for matches. I moved quickly past them as leather jacket cupped his hand round Ramón's cigarette. He followed me of course but I made it into Gran Vía before he could get at all close to me. The wide pavements were indeed crowded and there were police everywhere. The general movement was towards the Palace, but the smaller streets on the left which would have led there more quickly were blocked off. The crowd fed into the tail of the queue just short of the Santo Domingo Metro and I found myself in a file which, it appeared, contained two duchesses, without jewels, a retired surgeon and a retired general. For a time I assumed with them the upright bearing, the eyes glassily fixed on an imaginary point six inches above the head in front, and shuffled along thus to the manner born. But I was anxious too to see what had become of leather jacket and soon I was committing the solecism of peering all around me. Garish and bizarre, the several cinemas clustering round Santo Domingo displayed posters that would not change for a week or a month, no matter who died, whose funeral it was. *American Graffiti, Clockwork Orange*, and, live on stage, *Jesus Christ, Superstar*.

'The queue occupied one half of the carriageway. The pavements were now almost empty except for the *policía armada* at intervals and intersections. And sure enough, before long there he was, in front of me, on the pavement scanning the files of mourners as they passed him. He spotted me and flashed white teeth in something like a grin – I did not smile back.

'Five minutes later we rounded into Plaza de España, and, to my relief, the queue moved along the south side. A minute or two later and we were passing the steps of El Príncipe. I murmured apologies to my duchesses and generals and trotted up the steps into the congenial warmth of the foyer...'

33

Cockburn's room was less congenial. As he let Roberto in, Swivel podgy, with a towel round his waist, came out of the bathroom, rubbing his sparse hair with another. Clemann, fully dressed, was sitting at a table in the window watching the queue. The remains of a large Spanish hotel breakfast were scattered over the room.

'Come in,' said Clemann. 'You are lucky to find me here. Thanks to this... *show*,' he gestured scornfully at what was happening below – 'flights from Barajas are all delayed or cancelled. Well, what have you come to tell me?'

This was indeed the question. Should he tell the whole truth, some of it, none of it even? The important thing was to persuade Clemann to take the tapes off their hands and take on the danger that went with them. But could he do that? No doubt Clemann could take care of himself. No doubt McCabe had thought the same. And there remained the crisis of conscience he had felt at McCabe's cynical readiness to use the tapes even though forged. Clemann's use would be conditional on his acceptance of them as authentic and it would not be cynical. But could Roberto now allow him to market them in that way, write into history a falsehood?

Dumb with all this in his mind, he removed gloves and coat, groped for a chair.

Clemann, with compassion that was both Olympian

and reproving relieved him of the necessity of making a choice. 'We know you forged some if not all of your tapes. Señora González made one quite serious mistake. She underestimated Steve's attachment to me and the extent to which he was upset by her association with Gunter. He returned the night before last drunk but coherent with a tale of intimacy and collusion between you and González. I spent most of yesterday making enquiries, as far as the log jam on the Madrid telephone system allowed, and it now seems Josefina Constanza González is your daughter.'

This made an act of confession, if not contrition, easier. Roberto nodded his head emphatically, fingered a broken madeleine on the table in front of him, rejected it. 'Yes, yes. That is all just so. But there is something else you should know. McCabe came to my flat last night, having come to a similar conclusion, in spite of which he made a private bid for the tapes. He was shot as he left. Shot dead...'

'Jesus,' cried Swivel, and edged further into the room, away from doors and windows. Fat and wet, he looked very vulnerable.

'Oh shit!' hissed Cockburn, who was sitting on the edge of one of the beds.

Clemann was brisk. 'You had better tell me the whole story as briefly as you reasonably can.'

It was a brief account. Roberto quickly outlined how he had written a satirical play about the Peróns for Puig and Castillo, how Pepa had seen it and been impressed by Puig's impersonation; how she had approached them and revealed that she was Roberto's daughter whom he had not seen for twenty-five years and told them of her peripheral involvement in the sale of the first tapes; how Cockburn had been set up to believe Roberto was an independent expert on the Peróns. He skipped through the events of the previous week, but gave them a fuller account of McCabe's visit and murder.

Clemann asked: 'Why did you do all this? You do not

strike me as greedy or ambitious. I should have guessed you were too sensible to be merely a meddler.'

Roberto explained how for thirty years he had devoted his life and money to running radical bookshops. Life remained but the money had gone.

Clemann turned to Swivel who was now clothed in a scarlet silk dressing-gown.

'He should go to the police,' said Swivel. 'Immediately. And if he doesn't we should. We are in possession of facts the police should have. No doubt of it. No two ways.'

'Steve?'

Cockburn leant forward, passed fingers through the tarnished silver of his curly hair. 'No doubt from a narrowly legalistic point of . . . '

There was hysteria in Swivel's voice: 'Christ, Cockburn, it's not narrowly legalistic to suggest murders should be reported to the authorities.'

'All right. But I do rather take leave to wonder what will be achieved.'

Clemann: 'I take your point. This was the murder of a man working for the US State Department, possibly with a CIA control. On the State Department's behalf he was apparently conspiring to commit a fraud. Fairrie indicates it was a contract killing set up by one of the agencies the Nazis use to protect themselves, the sort of people who had López Rega shot. If that is the case the Spanish police will be totally ineffectual, their hands tied twice – by the CIA, and by the tolerance of fascism in the ruling cliques. The law may be served by reporting this to the police. Justice will not.'

Swivel shook his fat head in exasperation, unknotted and reknotted the silk belt round his waist.

Cockburn: 'And if this murder is reported we, you Peter, will be subjected to a lot of inconvenience. Form at least will require that we be asked to stay in Madrid at least during the preliminary enquiries. I imagine that would be a nuisance for you. It certainly would for me.'

'Hang on.' Swivel, on one side of the bed, twisted his head to bring part of Cockburn in view. 'I do find I have to ask myself this. To what extent is Cockburn's position one he has taken up out of undeclared motives of self-interest?'

'What the fuck are you talking about?'

'I imagine Josefina González's interests will also be served by hushing this up.'

'Oh come on. Come *on*.' Cockburn appealed to Clemann. 'You can't imagine I've got any thought of that in my mind. She set me up for this. I was the means through which she was to get her grubby fingers on your lucre. Anyway. Gunter is screwing her on a regular basis, he's a hell of a lot richer than I am and better at it too, I dare say.'

Roberto detected real spite directed at him behind this outburst. The whole business indeed was distasteful, like some sultan's divan where advisers vied with each other to offer what would best protect their favoured positions at the Sublime Porte. Except, he thought quirkily, in this case it's not the Sultan who is on the divan, but the advisers.

'Which brings us back to Gunter. What do you know about him, Fairrie?'

Roberto recapitulated what he had heard from Juan 'Evita' Castillo.

'Clearly,' said Clemann, 'there is every indication that he is a link between your tapes and Die Spinne.' He stood up, peered out of the window and down into the square. 'In the last decade lines have become very blurred in these areas. Nazis, financiers, arms-dealers, drug operators, the banks, the hierarchy of the Church, the Christian Democrats – one used to know one area from another, though recognising that an evil symbiosis existed between them. But now they're more locked together, tangled, as if disparate parts have come together to make – a monster. Your leather-jacketed friend is still there, and indeed there are now two of them. What we have to decide is what *do* we do. No, Henry, I am not going to the police.'

'In that case sit tight, and get the hell out as soon

as we can.'

'Which won't be for several hours yet, if not days.'

'So. Sit tight.'

'Yes indeed. I heard you. *We* have little option. What I meant was, how can we help Mr Fairrie, for it was, was it not, for help that he came.'

Silence. The murmur as of a sea distant and calm, of ten thousand well-shod feet shuffling, moving like a single organism.

Swivel let out air. 'Peter. This man tried very hard to sell you fraudulent goods. For one heck of a lot of money.'

'Yes, Henry. But his motives were not dishonourable. One may question the means, but that's an old question which no one has answered without being guilty of either blatant hypocrisy or overt brutality. So. How can we help him? It might be helpful to see if we can't put together a clearer picture of what he's up against. Many people might have an interest in suppressing or getting editorial control of these tapes. As was the case with the first lot. But most, CIA, *ABC*, even Peronists would murder as a third or fourth option. But I suspect Nazis alone would choose that option first. Now. At the first hearing of these tapes Cockburn tells me González played a tape cutting it off immediately before apparent revelations about Bormann. I imagine, Fairrie, you had a lot more of the same sort of thing.'

'Yes. A whole cassette. Ninety minutes.'

'But invented.'

'No. I believe not.' Roberto tried to master the agitation he felt. 'The chief source, I believe, was a Montonero exile in Madrid, in touch with Montoneros in Buenos Aires, Córdoba and so on. As you know, most of that movement are middle-class, or higher. Many families have been married into by Nazi *émigrés*. There were, after all, ten thousand of them or more. The Montoneros have built up a large, and I believe accurate dossier. What they lack is a means of publishing it. No one would touch it without adulterating it. Our tapes seemed a good outlet, and they gave us the information.'

'But no one heard that cassette beyond the introduction, apart from González, Puig, yourself and the Montonero source.'

'No.'

'Unless,' said Swivel, 'González played it to Gunter on the q.t.'

'She did play some tape to him, but not that one I'm sure. We made her very aware of the danger of it, of what might happen if anyone got wind of it apart from you.'

'Why play even the introduction then?' asked Cockburn.

'I'm sorry.' Roberto now sounded desperate. 'It was my idea as far as I remember. I wanted to impress you. I wanted to give you something that you would expect the *Sunday Times* to pay well for. Thus, to make sure you would get in touch with Mr Clemann.'

'Certainly that was well judged.' Clemann was dry. 'And no one else heard the rest of that tape?'

'No. I am certain of it.'

Clemann moved back to the window. 'Not even the Nazis would have committed murder on the strength of that small extract. Someone has leaked the rest of that tape. I suppose it has to be the Montonero who supplied the information in the first place.' He moved across the small room to the chimney breast and again perched his elbows on the high mantel. 'If, and it seems very likely, we are up against Die Spinne or some other Nazi agency, with the added possibility that they have infiltrated the very people you most trust, there is very little we can do about your safety until you can satisfy them that these tapes are destroyed. Except offer you asylum here.'

Swivel looked up sharply. 'Peter, I have to say this. If you do that you book a second room. Three in here is bad enough. Four would be impossible.'

Clemann appeared momentarily embarrassed. 'Well, I

don't see that as entirely necessary.'

'Come on, Peter.' This from Cockburn, who turned to Roberto. 'Peter has strict ideas about what is money well spent, and what is not. This room is booked for one person, but three of us are living in it...'

'That will do, Steve. I spend my money as I see fit. If you want me to pay for your accommodation in Madrid, and Henry's, you accept what I offer. Well, Fairrie?'

'There is Ramón to think of. He is still in Desengaño.'

'You got out. Using that show out there. You can get back the same way. You can come back with Puig too if you want.'

'I think,' said Roberto, 'I shall have to try something like that. I must first get back to Ramón. It was silly to leave him.'

He stood up, reached for hat, coat, muffler, gloves, put them on slowly. As he did he reflected that it had been a wasted visit. He was not quite clear about what he had hoped to achieve from it. Perhaps instant deployment of Clemann's wealth and power, US Cavalry style, to get Ramón and him out of Desengaño, safely guarded in armoured limousines. Clearly such an idea was pure fantasy. There was quite a lot to be said for Clemann. He used his wealth for broadly progressive causes, and rather more wisely than Roberto had used his. But he was after all Peter Clemann, not Clark Kent.

Clemann stood up too. 'Before you go I would like to return to one other matter.'

'Yes?'

'López Rega. Your daughter used his arrival and disappearance in Madrid to give her an explanation of the provenance of your forged tapes. This was an opportunistic device prompted by his arrival after your plot was under way?'

'Yes.'

'His arrival was reported in the newspapers?'

'Yes.'

'But do you not think it possible that he really did come to see her? We checked out that document giving her title to the contents of the safe deposit box, and the manager of the bank was adamant that it was genuine. So she really did see López Rega, who really did put something on deposit in that bank, or if not López, then someone else. Do you have a view on any of this?'

Roberto felt the grip of cold doubt and fear.

'I don't know. I really don't know. You see, for very obvious reasons we have kept as far apart as possible once things got under way.'

'I understand that. Now it appears there are five cassettes in that safe that have nothing to do with you and Ramón Puig. Is it not possible that those are what López Rega brought with him?'

'I don't know. It's possible. But I don't know.'

Clemann turned back to the window. 'Mr Fairrie, *if* those tapes, five of them, are what I think they are, I would be very interested, very interested indeed in acquiring them. Please bear that in mind. Steve, show Mr Fairrie down. I hope we'll meet again. Perhaps later today if you can manage that without undue risk.'

34

On the way down Roberto felt impelled to say: 'I am sorry, you know. Sorry for many things. Not least my daughter's behaviour towards you.'

Cockburn continued to look grim as he strode, chin up, dark eyes glittering, towards the lift. He jabbed the call button.

In the lift Roberto went on: 'I see now it was a very silly caper to invent, to involve others in. Very silly for amateur conspirators. My heart was never quite in it. I did not like the element of deception, the distortion of history. And now it has ended in tragedy. I find I can describe the murder of even a man like McCabe as tragic.'

They came into the warm, silent foyer, walked to revolving doors.

'I am horribly afraid the tragedy is not over. I only hope it will not involve Pepita.'

Cockburn stopped, hand on the door.

'She has Gunter to look after her.'

As Roberto entered the revolving door he felt it suddenly impelled from behind so he was almost ejected into the cold air.

Momentarily furious he almost said aloud: 'You *bastard*!'

Then he glanced down the steps, saw the leather jackets talking to the Guardia Civil on the other side of the road, and fear clutched again. Muttering '*Perdón señor, señora perdón*', he slipped into the river of icy privilege.

Nevertheless, it moved slowly, far more slowly even than before. For five minutes or so his mind juggled aimlessly yet fearfully with all the disparate elements in the mess he now saw himself to be in. He could not make them fit. Basically it came down to this: everyone, even apparently Gunter, from what Pepita had suggested, now seemed to know that the Perón tapes, his and Ramón's tapes, were a hoax, a fraud. Yet still McCabe, and now Clemann had been, were ready to buy if the five other cassettes were included in the bargain. And someone was ready to kill, had killed to make sure they were not sold. Clemann had suggested that the information, which 'Evita' had brought them, concerning Perón and the Nazis, was accurate and that that was what lay behind it all. If that was the case then 'Evita' or his source had betrayed them . . . or, there was no one else, Pepita, coerced by Gunter.

These were thoughts not to be faced and Roberto consciously pushed them from his mind, deliberately set out to recall the only other occasion he had attended a lying-in-state – though such is the way the unconscious mind works the choice of distraction was dictated by the fear that prompted it.

27 June 1952. Driven by a complex of emotions almost as unravellable as those he felt now, he had joined that particular queue at about half past three in the afternoon and then shuffled for two hours beneath his umbrella, in torrential cold rain, before reaching the portals of the Ministry of Labour.

That queue had been very different. It had been poor. Rain-soaked, it smelled – of wet heavy cloth, of unwashed armpits, of onion and garlic, above all of work. There had been some resentment at his presence: an Italian-looking docker from La Boca had suggested that those with their coats on, that is those who were not *decamisados*, had no

204

business there. Someone else had told the docker to be quiet: Roberto must be sincere, one of them, for all the real bastards were being driven in in large American limousines or the new Mercedes. If you had money, if you were a general, above all if you were a crook you did not queue.

Half-hearted bickering broke out about this but was silenced by the angry wailing of a nearly blind old woman, who claimed Evita had cured her eyesight just by touching...

Roberto had been accompanied by an acquaintance called Alfonso, about five years his junior, a law student from a poorish background – his father a modest wholesale dealer in vegetables. Alfonso, a member of the Argentinian CP was there, he said, because it was important that all cadres should understand the nature of the Evita phenomenon: only from a basis that included true comprehension of its nature would it be possible to build up objective class consciousness in the Buenos Aires proletariat.

Nevertheless, after they had climbed the long staircases of Ministry building to the columned rotunda of the auditorium and had at last seen the white, tilted casket, and peered through the reflecting glass at the painted doll framed in orchids, it was Alfonso who wept. Not Roberto, because for him a spell had been broken, the spell that had captivated Argentinians of every class apart from the oligarchy, the landowners, and the grandees amongst the generals. The doll was part of the myth and, whatever had been real in Eva had nothing to do with the myth, and it was the reality that had died. The doll and the myth remained – to be refuted, defused, exorcised.

And then something extraordinary had happened, for at that precise moment a corner of the curtain of the myth was tweaked, and a touch of reality showed past it. Just as he and Alfonso were moving on, impelled by the spaces in front of them and the solid thousands behind, the whole slow movement stopped, as it had a hundred times during their wet wearisome progress to this point, to allow some dignitary or whatever a privileged minute of farewell.

Three men in leather coats, with soft hats pulled over their faces, were let through a tall, white door to one side, and were ushered by a functionary to the front of the casket. They removed their hats. One, the shortest of them, took a step forward, and stood for a full minute with head bowed, only a yard from the doll so it seemed he could lean forward and kiss her back to life. He had a plump but strong face, receding black hair, thickish lips: so much Roberto clearly saw before he snapped back to join the men behind, and with both hands pulled the hat back firmly over head and face. Like a gangster in a film he twitched up the collar of his coat. They turned, did not exactly march, but walked swiftly, and were gone.

Alfonso's tears were gone too. He was white – with terror? Rage? He said nothing until they were in the rain-drenched street again, anonymous particles in a vast but disintegrating crowd.

'That,' he said at last, 'was Martin Bormann.'

This second queue moved on, wheeled beneath the tiny dancing snowflakes – the very old and the very sick always die when the weather is bad, thought Roberto – into the Plaza de la Armería, and the huge, ornate façade, one of the last and most assertive monuments in Baroque art, spread and climbed above them. Momentarily a tiny laugh bubbled in Roberto as he recalled those earlier and on the whole more likeable gangsters in history, the Bonaparte brothers. Napoleon handing the palace over to his elder brother Joseph had said wryly: 'Tu seras mieux logé que moi.' Then he realised how the crowds leaving the palace by only two exits dissolved instantly, just as that leaving the Ministry of Labour in Buenos Aires twenty-three years earlier had done, and the two leather jackets had only to wait at those narrow exits to pick him up.

206

35

An arrangement for military band of the slow march from Chopin's B flat minor sonata was, for Roberto, an act of vandalism. He silenced the radio, looked sightlessly out of his window at the corner of the Telefónica opposite.

PLAY AND RECORD:

'I suppose it has to be someone among the Montoneros. It could be "Evita". Why not? He's the only person apart from Ramón, Pepita and me who knew what was on the Nazi tape. He could be playing a double game. He generates the information from his Nazi friends and relations, then, through our tapes sells it back again. And Nazi friends he certainly does have. He slips like a snake from the *ambiente* of the exiles into the bourgeois world of Gunter and South American business with all its shady associates, and then back to the exiles. And he has money from somewhere. He supported Ramón as far as Ramón would let him.

'They quarrelled bitterly. Violently at times. He could, yes I believe he could, when drunk or doped or angry, permit Ramón's death... I think so.

'And he knew all about La Aguja. The Needle. Why is he called the Needle? Perhaps I'll know soon.

'Of course he may not be doing it for money. Like poor Becky he might very well be caught in some

207

dangerously ambiguous position. A relative under threat, something of that sort or evidence of terrorist activity strong enough to make the authorities here frightened enough to deport him.

'Becky. Poor soul. And... how lovely in her way. She was kind and warm to me. If, if, when La Aguja comes for me, and takes me, dear Lord... not too painfully, and not blasted to bloody pieces like McCabe, please no, I must try then to remember Becky, her long fingers caressing my neck, the warmth of her brown breasts...

'La Aguja.'

STOP.

As a very small boy, playing with friends whose father owned a hacienda in the Tucumán, he had poked with a stick into a hole where they knew a giant spider was lurking. They called it a tarantula, though in fact it was one of the *aviculariidae* or bird-eaters. With just the same horrid fascination he now moved wearily into the kitchen and pushed open the metal-framed frosted glass.

He should not have done it. The shock was almost a death blow.

They were framed by the lower window like puppets in a booth, a family group in a photograph frame: La Aguja standing, and Gunter too, both looking over Pepita's shoulder as she sat at the table and wrote something with a thin gold pen.

He closed the casement, and as he moved back, shaking his head with despair like a caged animal, his ears were mind-shatteringly assaulted with what sounded like a short burst of heavy machine-gun fire followed by a longer, continuing burst which became a deafening roar. For a moment the pale lemon sunlight on the corner of his desk went out, then the monster, black against the sky, a giant metal dragonfly, canted and, moving obliquely, soared briefly across his field of vision, and was gone. The dreadful clatter of its engine diminished, receded, became at last just another element in the subdued rumble of the expectant city.

Against it the nearness of a breath pulled in behind him, a yard behind him, had the force of an electric shock. Every muscle in Roberto's body tightened, including his heart, and terror rinsed his mouth.

'Where's Ramón?'

Roberto twisted, the cane chair creaked. Juan 'Evita' Castillo was in the doorway, dark hair swept back, face pale, anxious, above a denim jacket over a blue shirt with mother-of-pearl buttons, immaculate jeans, repeated: 'Where is he?' He still had his latchkey in his hand.

Roberto struggled to speak, half rose, twisting, pushing back the chair. 'Evita' gave the key an impatient shake.

'He's in the bath.'

'What?' Sharp black eyebrows drawn together in a frown.

'Dead... in the bath.'

The youth turned on flamenco heels, two, three steps across the hall brought him into the bathroom door. Roberto followed, just had time to take in the wardrobe, angled back from the door, then...

'Christ! Jesus fucking Christ,' and Juan 'Evita' went at him, hand drawn back, and then, bang, bang, slapped the old man hard, twice, across the face. Roberto turned, tried to get back to his room, but was caught by the collar, twisted and hit again. His glasses, already askew and slipping, went with the backhand to the wall, to the floor.

'How? HOW?' Juan's voice a scream and a shout.

'Yesterday. Morning. I don't know...'

Juan pushed Roberto into his room, tumbled him on to the bed and sat on the cane chair. Piecemeal and confused some of what had happened during the previous twenty-four hours was dragged out. When Roberto came to describe how he had got past the leather jacket to get out of the house and into the street, into Gran Vía, Juan suddenly smashed his fist into the confusion of papers, pencils,

.apes on the desk.

'You bastard sons of donkeys...' Hands shaking he found a pack of Chesterfield in the breast pocket of his jacket. He struggled with a lighter, then: 'Shit. Get me a brandy.'

Roberto, dabbing a nose that bled and a bruised lip, groping almost sightlessly in the dark passage, but able to see in the kitchen, poured out the last of the Osborne, gulped back one for himself.

'Those leather jackets as you call them are mine. When I knew La Aguja was around I found them, and paid them to keep watch on you. On you and Ramón. And when you went out they both followed you. They must have thought Ramón would be... safe... here.' And suddenly he broke, his hands went to his face, seemed almost to be clawing it, and he sobbed and sobbed, gasping for air between each spasm, and rocking from side to side in the creaking chair. Roberto watched, then stubbed out the smouldering cigarette, put an arm around the boy, he was no more than that, and beneath the jacket bird-thin, tried to get him to drink brandy.

Juan shrugged him off but took the brandy, looked up at him. 'Did they torture him?'

Roberto's eyes flinched away.

Juan nodded. 'They'd want to know... all about the tapes. Jesus, I hope he told them quickly.' It seemed the storm of grief would return but he bit his lip, clenched fists, pushed himself upright, ran hands across his face, through his hair.

'We must do something for him. How could you leave him?'

He went back into the bathroom. Roberto, reluctantly, followed. Juan stooped, knelt, tenderly peeled the obscene Perón mask from his lover's head, then kissed his lips.

'Get towels. Spread them on his bed.'

Sick at the horror of it all, but now deeply ashamed that he had done nothing, Roberto stumbled blindly about the flat, did as he was told. He found four largish towels, all already damp and threadbare.

'You must help me. He is too heavy. And he is still stiff, though beginning to give. We'll manage.'

He had his arm round Ramón's back.

'Take his legs. Under the knees.'

The body was icy, the cold a shock. Roberto felt a wave of appalling pity, followed by a terrible determination not to slip, not to drop him, not to inflict further humiliation beyond the humiliation of death on his friend. Even if it meant ruptures, or a heart attack.

The foul cold water cascaded as they lifted, splashed on and about them. Almost he slipped.

The body would not straighten, would not lie easily on its back. Tenderly they allowed it to go on its side. Then Juan wiped it clean with the towels, took them back to the bathroom. He took a sheet from Roberto's bed and draped it over the body. For a moment they both looked down at it. In spite of the intensity and depth of what he had felt, Roberto's quirky sense of the rational reasserted itself in a corner of his mind. The hair in the beard had grown a little. Ramón never let it get beyond a stubble. And the eyes, like those of the dead Caudillo, were not quite shut. It was, when all was said and done, a corpse.

Gently Juan drew the sheet over the head.

'In the bath he looked like a dead dictator. Lying in state. This is better.' He breathed in deeply, let out a long sigh, and said, peremptorily: 'Leave us.'

Roberto, gratefully, went.

Brandy, a beating, the effort of moving Ramón threatened to finish processes begun forty-eight hours or more earlier. The worst of all was the vision of Pepita with Gunter and Betelmann in the room below. All part of Clemann's monster, part of the same organism. What romantic nonsense had led him to believe any otherwise? Nausea which retching would not relieve, a sandbag heaviness in every limb and joint, tunnel vision that flickered, and an evil weariness of the soul that would have led to suicide if he had the strength to do it descended upon him. He heard Juan moving, then a door clicked, and he believed he had gone and was relieved. At least La Aguja would have to look for him. Presently he pulled his legs up, sank back, and thumb in mouth, eyes open, waited.

Twenty minutes later, perhaps, he heard again the click of a key in the outside door, steps, then his own door opened. Pepita, and behind her La Aguja. She dropped to her knees beside him, tried to cradle his head in her arms. She wept. 'Papa, Papa, what have I done to you? What have we done to each other.' La Aguja took the cane chair, twisted it so he could see them. In podgy white hands he held, across his knees, the large automatic pistol he had used to kill McCabe.

After a time Roberto pulled himself up into a sitting position with his back against the bars of the bed, his head on the wall, and took Pepita's head in his lap. He stroked her gently and peered at the indistinct figure that blocked out the light from the window. With an effort he focused. Without glasses his vision was long, nothing nearer than two metres was distinct.

A fat pasty face, bad teeth which occasionally their owner picked, a suit that was overfilled, a black tie. Many people wore black ties during those days after Franco's death, but Roberto felt La Aguja wore one all the time.

'You are going to kill us?' Then, as the horror became more certain: 'Both of us?'

'Sí.'

Beneath his hand he felt Pepita's spasm, and he stroked her more urgently. Crazily he relished the fineness of her disordered hair and the warmth of her head and shoulders in the pit of his stomach, the fragrance of her perfume and body. At least it was clear the betrayal he had feared was not as complete as he had thought. Perhaps there had been no betrayal at all.

'You should not keep us waiting.'

'I am not to do it until this business in the Cortes is over and the streets are open again.' The voice was squeaky, almost unbroken. 'Your bodies and the one in the bath will have to be moved.'

'What will you do with them?'

'One of the contractors for the development at Colón owes us. Ten cement tankers go into the foundations on Monday. Should have been today.' He now began to bite the nails of one hand. Then he giggled: 'You'll have good company. López Rega, El Brujo, is already there.'

Roberto blinked, closed his eyes, clenched his whole body except the hand that stroked his daughter, tried to force himself out of despair and into thought, action even.

'You must kill me because I saw you kill the American. But why her?'

The fat man shrugged. 'I do what I am paid to do.'

'I think you should at least contact your employers and allow her to question... She has assets they are interested in. I think they must in fact be tapes López Rega brought with him. Everything dangerous that López was to your employers still exists on those tapes.'

Pepita moaned, twisted a little. 'It's no use, Papa. No use. Together they made me write an authority for Enrico. So he can collect the tapes from the bank. He did nothing for me, nothing... ' Again she began to sob. Outside, the bell down the road slowly tolled twelve. She continued to sob. Clearly the noise irritated La Aguja. He reached out, dabbed a finger at Roberto's radio.

A measured voice, pitched a little higher than its normal level, filled a round space, terraced seats beneath a small dome, silent except for a distant cough or two...

'*La justicia es el supuesto para la libertad con dignidad... Insistamos en la construcción de un orden justo, un orden donde tanto la actividad público como la privada se hallen bajo la salvaguardia judiccional.*'

213

In spite of everything Roberto's back stiffened, a light began to glitter in his eye. With his head almost jauntily set on one side he strained to catch the words. As if sensing it was what he wanted, Pepita fell silent. And what *was* this? Public activity, that is the activity of the State, should be as subject to the law as private activity? But that is openly acknowledging that under the old regime that was not the case!

'A just order allows the recognition of regional differences... The King seeks to be King of everyone, and that means each one in his own culture, his own history, his own tradition.' So, an end to Castilian cultural hegemony over Basques, Catalans, Andalusians.

'*Una sociedad libre y moderna requiere la participación de todos en los foros de decisión...* ' Was it imagination or did the hush deepen over a parliament packed with Franco's henchmen? Certainly, thought Roberto, there is no likelihood of rapturous applause... the participation of *everybody*? That's democracy, of a sort. And now... He's Catholic, respects the Church. But respect for the dignity of the person implies the principle of religious liberty... *Libre*... *Libertad*, come on, Juan Carlos, that's no sort of language to use with that old monster still above ground.

Roberto felt a lightening of his soul as the speech moved on, a pricking of tears. Was this the suppressed bourgeois in him, the unreconstituted liberal humanist that was moved thus by the voice of a *king*?

Click and silence. La Aguja killed the King, or the voice at any rate. There were two blobs of colour on the assassin's cheeks, and savagely he pulled back the breech of his gun, cocked it. 'King?' It was almost a squawk. 'I give him six weeks.'

Roberto slumped back, resumed his weary stroking of Pepita's hair, felt the stupid tears on his cheeks — 'Wipe thine eyes,' he murmured, 'the good years shall devour them, ere they shall make us weep.'

La Aguja stirred, glanced at his watch, felt in his pockets. Metal clinked, through Roberto's broken vision something glittered, flashed in the space between them, landed chunkily on the bed. Handcuffs.

'Fasten one cuff of one pair to your left wrist, let the other cuff hang. Then use your left hand to fasten the second pair to your right wrist and the other half to the woman's right wrist.'

'Is this... ?'

The gun lifted. 'Do as you are told. This will be painless and clean. No mess. Otherwise I shoot you, and no matter what you see at the cinemas that is not always quick, and is always dirty.'

Ratchets snickered. The metal was not cold, had been in the fat man's pocket. Roberto's nausea returned.

Suddenly, so it made him jump, renewed the flavour of fear in his mouth, the assassin moved – he snapped the remaining cuff on to the metal upright of the bedstead. Roberto caught the sourness of his breath. La Aguja, back at the table, placed the gun carefully at his elbow and took two packets from his coat pocket. Working briskly he peeled oiled brown paper from them, opened the lids of dark blue, solidly made cardboard boxes, disclosed a phial and a hypodermic syringe. He pierced the rubber seal on the phial, held it up, sucked a colourless liquid from one to the other.

'Pentobarbitone,' he said. 'Vets use it for killing unwanted or suffering pets. It is very quick and there is no pain.'

Roberto strove to gentle Pepita, but found the most he could do was lace his fingers with hers.

'I shall struggle.'

'That would be foolish. For if you do I shoot you instead. Perhaps in the stomach.'

He withdrew the needle from the phial. He was breathing faster now, almost panting. The cane creaked as with his left hand he pushed down on the arm and his body again began to fill the light. The right hand held the loaded syringe point up, like a torch. Perhaps, Roberto thought, someone will listen to my tapes. All of them.

And there, as the door opened, La Aguja froze, his grey face suddenly ashen, his mouth dropped open, the bottom lip quivering. As if, as they say, he had seen a ghost.

Which, in effect, he had.

Eva María Duarte de Perón, blonde hair swept back to a bun, rhinestones flashing beneath her ears, a rose-coloured ball-gown that glittered with gems and sequins except where a blue and white silk sash covered them, faced him, and pointed the small silver pistol at him. Still holding the syringe La Aguja sank to his knees crossing himself repeatedly with his free hand. An Act of Contrition, or a superstitious attempt to placate the powers of evil? Eva shot him, through one lens of his glasses, in the left eye. Death was not quick. Three more shots, placed behind the left ear were needed before the terrifying pumping of blood ceased.

36

Juan 'Evita' Castillo had not only resource, but resources too. On Saturday, the day of Franco's funeral,
when Pinochet was again cheered by the *Azules*, the
veterans who had fought for Hitler on the Russian front,
and Falange hymns in the Valley of the Fallen drowned out
the speakered order of the service, Roberto and Pepita were
driven from Vellas Vistas where they had spent the night,
to Salamanca.

It was a good place to hide: one of the most right-wing
cities in Spain, it had been the rebel headquarters in 1936
before Franco moved to Burgos. Bormann stayed there off
and on between 1945 and 1948. Perhaps for this reason the
IRA bombers who blew up Carrero Blanco for the Basques
in 1973, also lay low here before crossing into Portugal.

Roberto and Pepita stayed with a part-time teacher in
the English Department of the University who frequently
lent her spare room to transient refugees of one sort or
another. She was writing a thesis on Arnold Wesker, a left-
ish British playwright of the sixties. She had a son, aged
two and a half, who walked about the flat without a nappy
and was pursued by a maid with a potty. Roberto helped
her with the thesis, Pepita with the little boy, therapy for
both of them. There was a husband, also an academic, but
not much in evidence, except at nine o'clock in the evening
when he came into the living-room to listen to the BBC

World News in Spanish, and everyone had to keep quiet. It was a domestic time. Roberto and Pepita got to know each other and planned to pool all their resources: $20,000 from McCabe, over $4,400 altogether from Clemann, and another seventeen from the surrender of the lease on Pepita's flat and the sale of jewellery and furs she no longer much liked, and so restart yet again a Fairrie Radical Bookshop. They rather hoped it might be somewhere near the Rue de Rennes in Paris.

Snow fell. Freezing fog descended. Christmas came and they were feasted by their host's family through midnight on shellfish, sucking-pig and a Christmas pudding sent by one of her English friends. At the end Roberto accepted a *Romeo y Julieta* from Havana, enjoyed it enormously, and regretted it for four days. It took that long for the flavour, growing steadily nastier all the time, to leave his mouth. He had his revenge. He taught the infant to chant *Juan Carlos, Juan Carlos, Juan Carlos* and *Viva El Rey.*

On the day before New Year's Eve, in the late afternoon with dusk gathering, Roberto and his daughter wandered through the snow-clad city, came to the small square where a bronze philosopher tried vainly to stride off his plinth. Unamuno, Rector of the University. As a writer and thinker he was by no means a leftie, but when Franco came and made his university the headquarters of a rebel army, Unamuno made a public attack on the rebellion and the morals of fascism. A little later he died. Some say that he fell asleep over a round bowl of glowing charcoal, that his feet were burned, and he died from the gangrene that followed. Others of course said Franco did it. Who knows?

Roberto told the story to Pepa as they sat on a bench from which he had cleared the snow.

'I think,' he said, 'my moustache is icing up.'

'It is.'

So too were the plane tree saplings. The bobbled seed-cases that hung from their twigs looked like Christmas baubles.

Suddenly, without immediate premeditation he took a plunge he had been fearing to make for a week or more.

'López Rega, El Brujo,' he said, 'really did come to you?'

'Yes.'

'It must have seemed a heaven-sent opportunity.'

'Hardly heaven-sent.' She laughed a little. 'Opportune certainly.'

'And he actually did give you tapes of his own. Those five cassettes. And you put them in the vault with ours.'

'Yes.' She had stiffened, was defensive. 'I'm cold. Let's go back. Or to a café.'

They trudged through snow to one of the grand cafés in the Plaza Mayor – the loveliest square in the world, a rococo glory in rose and peach coloured stone, made yet more magical by snow. They sat in a window, ate cinnamon-flavoured biscuits with foamy espresso coffee.

'Did he say what was on the tapes?'

'Yes.'

He waited.

She went on: 'They were copies made from the Sassen tapes.'

He looked out. Bronze lamp-posts stood black against the white and rose. Windows glowed beneath the arcades. Children threw snowballs.

'Dear Lord. The Devil.'

Pepa's face was white above the sable she had kept, white but made-up, and so clownish, a tragic clown.

'Do you know what the Sassen tapes are?' he asked her.

'I didn't then. I know a bit more now.'

'They were tapes made by Eichmann not long before he was kidnapped. They were recorded by a Dutch Nazi journalist called Sassen. Transcripts went to Israel. They were a very full account of Eichmann's part in the Holocaust. The tapes were sold, to *Time-Life*, I think. But not all of them. Sassen refused to part with five of them, the last five, which gave a very full account of Bormann's association with the Peróns, between 1945 and 1955, and went on with the story of the German emigration to our country, right through to 1960. They very possibly indicated where the Nazi treasure was realised and invested. If that is the case, then with those tapes you could trace the assets of a hundred apparently reputable concerns back to Bormann and Hitler, and show that bankers, company chairmen and the rest may often know even now the ultimate source of their wealth. Sassen never sold those tapes. And anyone who ever got close to Bormann, or the secrets of the finances of the Fourth Reich, got killed. That is why Sassen kept those tapes.'

Roberto looked out over the square, and picked at imaginary crumbs.

'I suppose,' he went on, 'López Rega, a Chief of SIDE and the other security organisations, got his hands on them. No doubt he thought they were insurance. But always with Bormann that sort of thing becomes a death warrant. Damn near ours.'

Pepa looked down. 'I'm sorry.'

Roberto let out a sigh full of heartache. 'Ramón's death warrant.'

She looked up, eyes suddenly flaming. 'All right. But don't blame me, or yourself. He knew what he was doing.'

'He did?'

'Of course. Everything about the Nazis in your tapes that he recorded, came from the Sassen tapes. Not from Montoneros, or "Evita", nothing like that. We listened to the Sassen tapes, fed the material to you, you rewrote them as if Perón was speaking, and Ramón recorded them. He knew what he was doing.'

'But why did you not tell me?'

'First, because you would have suspected that we did not have the same confidence in your forgeries as you had.

Second, because we knew you would say it was too dangerous, that you would stop us from going ahead. So, don't blame me. It was, in any case, an accident.'

'An accident?'

'Gunter told me. La Aguja broke into the flat. He was to persuade Ramón, or you if you were there, to tell the truth about the tapes. He had heard... something, I don't know what, that finally convinced him that what we... I was really selling was the Sassen tapes. Anyway, when La Aguja got in he found Ramón already in the bath, with the fire beside him...'

'And the Perón mask on?'

'You know he liked to fool with that mask. Probably he was about to record your new script. He was being Perón as part of his preparation...'

'In the bath?'

She flashed back at him: 'Yes. Why not? Whatever else, you must admit Ramón was a bit *weird*. Anyway La Aguja threatened to drop the fire in if he would not talk. But far from talking he tried to resist, to fight for it, and La Aguja dropped the fire in, and that was that. It gave La Aguja a scare, what with the wet floor and everything he got quite a nasty shock himself. Which was why he left.'

Roberto crumbled his biscuit and looked out at heavy flakes of snow floating like feathers into the beauty of the square.

'It makes no difference,' he said, 'how he died.'

On one day in the first week of the New Year an Argentinian student they knew, a friend of Juan's, came for them. He had a Seat 127, quite new, and told them he was to take them to the French frontier. They were as safe now as they were likely to be.

'How so?'

The youth unfolded a newspaper cutting from his wallet.

Roberto read it. Enrico Gunter, Argentinian business-

221

man, Knight of St Columbus, pillar of Hispano-American society in Madrid, had been shot dead in the street outside his office in Arguelles. The police were concentrating their enquiries amongst the communities of left-wing exiles... Roberto made an effort and became shocked. After sixty-five years living in the twentieth century he was still determined to be shocked by murder. But his main feeling was of relief.

He passed it to Pepita. To his consternation she went pale, her eyes filled, her body was racked with sobs. For two hours she was unconsolable. He remonstrated. Gunter had been a thug, a bully, a cheat, a criminal – perhaps he had ordered their murder, certainly he had countenanced it. But... 'He was my lover,' she moaned.

By morning, when they were to leave, she was recovered. She had had, Roberto reflected with pompous wisdom, sufficiently few lovers for the act of physical union still to create deep bonds, leave its mark. But enough lovers for the bond to be a pretty flimsy business.

They left Salamanca before dawn, were driven in the Seat through the persisting freezing fog at alarming speeds with visibility often less than ten metres, up the Great Road through Valladolid, Burgos, Vitoria, and at nightfall over the Tolosa pass where the fog turned to rain. In a hotel in Irún they spent their last night in Spain.

The trains north were packed with migrant Portuguese and Spanish workers returning to industrial Europe after the Christmas break. No bookable seats were available until three o'clock in the afternoon. They took a taxi to Fuentarrabia and had a seafood lunch. After the awfulness of freezing fog and snow the Atlantic weather was mild, almost balmy.

Pepita left Roberto on a bench from which he could gaze across the estuary, and went off to do some last-minute shopping. The atmosphere was pearly. Why go further than St Jean de Luz, or Biarritz? Basques buy left-wing books. But through the haze he could see the gabled villas painted red and green, and saw them as suburban, provincial. No. It would have to be Paris. At thirty-one Pepita was not ready for the provincial life. Nor perhaps was he. But it was a good corner of the world to settle in, no doubt of that. Restlessly he recrossed his legs, and questions reasserted themselves that he had not dared face for weeks.

Pepita came back. She carried two plastic bags. Vichy cosmetics, made under licence in Spain where they cost just over half what they cost in France.

He asked her: 'Gunter and McCabe knew more about that first tape we played than just the extract they heard. How?'

'Do you think I told them?'

Pretty as ever. His daughter – newly discovered. King Lear and Cordelia, or rather Pericles and Marina.

'No.'

'You would rather that I had not?'

'Yes.'

'It would have been sensible of me to tell them what was on that tape.'

'Not sensible. Very dangerous.'

She tossed back the auburn hair that reminded him of her mother.

'Listen. You remember when we played that tape in the Banco de la Victoria de los Angeles?'

'Yes.'

'Think back. Visualise it.'

'I am doing that.' Prawn fishers were pushing complex rafts or rigs into the estuary of the river that separates Spain from France. The tide had changed. Cirrus overhead promised cold weather even here, tomorrow perhaps. The atmosphere had cleared a little and La Grande Rhune, a volcanically shaped peak to his right, to the east, the first of the Pyrenees, loomed a little through the haze.

'Well?'

'Tell me.'

'Herzer lit Cockburn's cigarette.'

223

'Yes.'

'And... the rain fell.'

He laughed – why not?

'And we all rushed about, and she picked up the tape-recorder.'

'And the tape?'

'Yes.'

A long pause.

'Did you see her do this?'

'No. But I realised someone had taken it, and she only really had the opportunity.'

'And you said nothing.'

A glassy wave from the Atlantic nudged the ripples of the river. Raucous seagulls wheeled and dived.

'Why not?'

'Papa. We had to *advertise*.'

'And she brought it back the day you played it to the Germans and through her the world and his wife knew what we had. And those really in the know would have pieced together that what we were really advertising was the Sassen tapes.'

'That's right.'

And, he thought, the one doubt in their minds was resolved when I convinced Becky that the 'Perón' tapes really were forged. Up until then it had always been possible that the detailed information on how the money of the Third Reich has been set to work like a virus throughout the financial centres of the West, with the declared purpose of creating a Fourth, came from Perón himself. But once those tapes were known to be forged, then the question became – where had the accurate and lethal information on them come from?

The most likely known source was the five tapes Eichmann recorded for Sassen that Sassen never sold. And one man had briefly held the sort of power needed to get hold of them and use them for his own ends: López Rega.

'It must have been a shock when Beck... Madame

Herzer mentioned the Sassen tapes in your apartment. After the rainfall in the vault. I mean... at that point no one was meant to know they were what it was all about.'

'Yes. Yes, it was.'

'Do you think she knew... even then?'

'I don't think so. They would have moved more quickly, with more certainty, if that had been the case. But for them it was perhaps already a remote possibility and she was, what do the English say?'

'Flying a kite?'

'Flying a kite.'

He reflected. 'You did well then. You covered up ... bravely.'

She squeezed his hand. Slowly she was learning to forgive the father who had deserted her when she was four years old. Deserted? Her mother's version. He was a nice man. They could get on.

Meanwhile Roberto continued to dwell on Becky Herzer's role.

As soon as Herzer reported to whomever was directing her, that the Perón tapes were forged and that person redirected Gunter, presumably sometime early in the night Franco died, then everything changed.

'That night I was at your apartment. Did Gunter receive a phone call?'

'I think he did. Yes.'

'Before he phoned Betelmann, told him to contact and follow me?'

'I think so.'

He watched the gulls, the sea, and the mountains, looked nervously at his watch. A train, after all, to be caught. Becky, warm, brown, deceiving, welcoming, lovely. Deceiving and ultimately, though she could not have known how things would turn out, murderous. He felt disenchanted. *Desengaño*.

'She was controlled by the Nazis. Not Gunter. Someone above both of them. But McCabe too?'

'I think so. She had this background. Something in her past. Just as likely the CIA knew about it as anyone else.'

'Yes.' A thought occurred to him. 'Did *you* ask her to Madrid? To advertise?'

'No. I think Enrico... Gunter must have done. Or perhaps this person you go on about who you say was behind Gunter.'

He shuddered. Die Spinne. The Spider. Stupid, ugly, melodramatic name.

'What's the matter?'

'Nothing.'

He stood up, picked up the Vichy bags. They would be hunted for what they knew. Pepita had heard, actually heard the Sassen tapes. Roberto knew their contents in detail.

'We don't,' he said, 'have to go to Paris.'

'We don't have to open a bookshop.'

'We could make it a sweet shop... a *confiserie*, in Biarritz.'

'Or a boutique.' Then, suddenly excited: 'Both perhaps. A *confiserie* on one side, silk scarves on the other.'

He looked back at the ocean and the estuary, sat down again and she sat beside him.

'Why not?' he asked. 'Why should anyone look for us in Biarritz or St Jean de Luz? I think perhaps, I prefer St Jean de Luz. But will it make money? Harrogate Real Old Toffee. Barker and Dobson humbugs. *Spécialités de la maison*.'

'Yves Saint Laurent. You can sell Chanel dresses off the peg now, you know. At any rate it will do better than a *bookshop*.' This said with a touch of scorn. Then she turned to him, greenish eyes above the sable, finding his, holding them. 'And never need we be broke. We have insurance.'

'We have?'

'Sure. Of course. *Bien entendu. Claro.* I copied the Sassen tapes. It's very easy now, you know. Well within the capabilities of my Akai music centre. I have them in this handbag.'

'You do?'

'And Clemann will buy. If we want him to.'

'Oh . . . The Devil!'

Blank with the never-ending horror of it all he watched herring gulls dive and scoop at the shifting flotsam where tide fought river.

He squeezed her hand, sighed.